Making Room

Critical Praise for the books of Djelloul Marbrook

Artemisia's Wolf (title story, *A Warding Circle*)

... successfully blends humor and satire (and perhaps even a touch of magic realism) into its short length ... an engrossing story, but what might strike the reader most throughout the book is its infusion of breathtaking poetry... a stunning rebuke to notoriously misogynist subcultures like the New York art scene, showing us just how hard it is for a young woman to be judged on her creative talent alone.

—Tommy Zurhellen, *Hudson River Valley Review*

Saraceno

... Djelloul Marbrook writes dialogue that not only entertains with an intoxicating clickety-clack, but also packs a truth about low-life mob culture *The Sopranos* only hints at. You can practically smell the anisette and filling-station coffee.

—Dan Baum, author of *Gun Guys* (2013), *Nine Lives: Mystery, Magic, Death and Life in New Orleans* (2009) and others

... a good ear for crackling dialogue ... I love Marbrook's crude, raw music of the streets. The notes are authentic and on target ...

—Sam Coale, *The Providence (RI) Journal*

... an entirely new variety of gangster tale ... a Mafia story sculpted with the most refined of sensibilities from the clay of high art and philosophy ... the kind of writer I take real pleasure in discovering ... a mature artist whose rich body of work is finally coming to light.

—Brent Robison, editor, *Prima Materia*

Alice Miller's Room (title story, *Making Room*)

This enchanting novella is a delicately wrought homage to Jung's famous principle of meaningful coincidence...

—*Breakfast All Day*, UK

... the story draws us into that mysterious and terrifying realm where the heart will have its say and all who enter leave transformed...

—Dr. Patricia L. Divine

Mean Bastards Making Nice

I love it. I admire it. It is you at your best.

—Novelist Gail Godwin on "The Pain of Wearing Our Faces"

Guest Boy

... it is in books like this that I seek answers and guidance as I travel my own path to enlightenment and contentment. This book opened a struggle in me ...

—Isla McKetta, editor, *A Geography of Reading*

Making Room

Baltimore Stories

Djelloul Marbrook

LEAKY BOOT PRESS

Making Room
by Djelloul Marbrook

First published in 2017 by
Leaky Boot Press
http://www.leakyboot.com

ISBN: 978-1-909849-29-7

For the indomitable people of Baltimore, Maryland

Acknowledgments

The title story of *Making Room* was first published as "Alice Miller's Room," an e-book, by Online Originals (London, UK) in 1999.

"The Sandman's Art" was published in *Prima Materia* (New York) ,Vol. 1, in 2002.

"The Fake Delacroix" appeared in *Breakfast All Day* (London, UK., and Dieppe, France), in issue 4.

"Charm City" appeared in *Potomac Review* (Maryland) in the late 1990s and won an honorable mention from *New Millennium Writings* in 2007.

"Otley" won an honorable mention from *New Millennium Writings* in 2008.

"The Year Harry Retired" won an honorable mention from *New Millennium Writings* in 2016.

Contents

Making Room

Others might contemplate such an act and dissuade themselves, but Paolo prayed at synchronicity's altar, which is why that Thursday his one-inch display ad appeared in the Homes section of *The Baltimore Sun.*

> ALICE MILLER—If you value her work and would like to create a magical room for the little person in your care, call Paolo Maio, (301) 271-8691.

The right patron would appear. If not, it was the wrong time and he would breathe life into his next idea. That he'd not been born to the realms of the Sforzas and Viscontis was hardly worth reflection, so intent was he on his inquiries into the nature of others. In time his face bore his question—Who are you?—and it amazed his friend and patron, Matthew Pieto, how many people troubled to tell him. But that was not his gift. His gift was that, having told Paolo who they were, they felt as if they'd acquired a ciphered account in a Swiss bank.

Dr. Natalya Yasdarov had read Alice Miller's books, was in fact the Swiss psychiatrist's conscious disciple, although it would have been news to Alice Miller, and when she saw Paolo's ad she laughed with pleasure. "Oh my, I wonder who he is!" Ordinarily Natalya wouldn't have been reading the Homes section, but she was renovating the old nickel-brick house on North Charles Street inherited from her aunt. Natalya wanted her 11-month-old nephew—no, her son—to have a respectable home.

She thought she'd been dreaming about the fey ad—"a magical room for the little person in your care"—as she sat in the kitchen sipping her second cup of coffee and watching Sacha dip his waterproof book in his cereal before munching on it.

She felt her hand reaching for the phone.

"Mr. Maio, my name is Natalya Yasdarov, I saw your ad in the paper..."

"That's a wonderful name. Are you Russian?"

"Sort of, yes."

"I'm sort of Italian."

"Actually I'm sort of confused—about your ad, I mean, but I found it intriguing. I've read Alice Miller, but what does she have to do with interior design?"

"I'll send you my vita. Then, if you like, we can meet."

"Yes, but what do you want to do?"

"Something truly wonderful. I'll just charge you for the materials. I really want to do it. Maybe it sounds a little crazy, but let me come tell you."

"It sounds a lot crazy, but crazy is my specialty."

They liked the humor in each other's voices and made a date to meet that evening. All day she found her lips starting to form his name, Paolo Maio, a name she liked very much. What would he be like? Serio: Vittorio Gassmann; comico: Giancarlo Giannini.

As he got out of his white pickup truck she saw a tall, precariously strung-together man in his late thirties perhaps, his pale blond hair flopping in the night wind. He had on white coveralls festooned with pockets and tool loops and a white dress shirt spattered with paints of many colors. Standing at the door in a pale blue tunic drawn in by a white scarf, she found herself smiling in amusement.

"Natalya Yasdarov?"

"Paolo Maio, I presume."

His cerulean eyes haunted his white eyelashes. His gaze seemed not merely direct; rather the cones and rods seemed to work at taking her in.

"I saw you in a painting in the Uffizi, I'm glad to see you looking happier."

"I looked unhappy?" She was enjoying herself.

"Bummed out. Father trouble probably. I mean, you looked virginal."

"What does virginal look like, Mr. Maio? Uh"—she held her hand up—"don't answer, I don't think I want to have this conversation with a stranger."

Paolo smiled as if he understood perfectly and wasn't in the least rebuffed.

"This room," she started again, "what have you in mind? No, wait a minute, who are you, I mean what do you do? I know of course people are not what they do, but we have to start somewhere besides the Uffizi, don't we?"

"If you think about Alice Miller you know a lot about what's wrong with the world. It seems to me it would be very reassuring to a child to make a brand new world of it, instead of just painting a room and putting goofy kiddy toys in it. It would be telling the child, 'You count, you're safe, the way you see things counts'."

Natalya had led him into the kitchen. She wished he hadn't stopped. She'd felt herself lolling comfortably among his words. "Please don't stop."

"I want to make a room filled with secret compartments, light shows hidden behind moveable panels, machinery moving in walls, like naked clockworks, villages recessed between the studs of the wall, a bed that rises to the ceiling and is surrounded in a beautiful tent when it's lowered. A lot would depend on whether the child is a girl or a boy."

"A boy, eleven months old."

"I'm an artist and a sculptor. My studio is down on South Broadway. I get these ideas."

"I see. Well, I get them too, but I never see my work finished. I'm a psychiatrist."

"A healer."

"No, not really. I think I show people how to heal themselves. They have to do the work."

"The hard part."

"Oh yes. Tell me how you got this idea?"

"It sort of filtered into place in my head one day when I was in Hutzler's buying a shirt to wear to an opening in New York. There was this couple with two kids, a girl and a boy. The father had spatially divorced them, you know, like he just happened to be standing there. The mother was pushing the girl in a stroller, and the stroller kept folding up because it hadn't been lock-set, and the boy kept tugging at her, he wanted to go somewhere. Then right out of the blue she backhands the kid. Pearl Harbor, wham! He starts yowling and she says, Are you gonna get it when we get home! In other words, his home is not safe for him, it's the place where he's gonna get it. He can't trust his parents. I lost it. I walked up to the mother and said, How would you like it if somebody hurt and humiliated you in public like that? She didn't know what to say. But the father says to me, Is this any of your business? I say, It's your business. He's madder at me than at what happened, so we eyeball each other until Mama hauls him off. I was pretty ashamed of myself."

"Why? You were right."

"The world's unsafe for children—if Alice Miller had said that everyone would have agreed, but she said their parents are unsafe, the kids can't trust their custodians, so how can they ever trust anyone?"

What a lovely man. How strange to meet him under the circumstances of her life, Sacha's life. She wondered what to say. "Uh, when you met me at the Uffizi, did I look foreign perhaps?"

He seemed puzzled.

"I'm a Jew." Why on earth did she feel compelled to say that?

"Ah, like the mother of God," he said with a relieved smile. "Why did you ask that?"

This was the moment to decide how their relationship might work, its demeanor. "I was at a loss for words."

"Oh. That happens to me all the time."

"And what do you do?"

"Paint. What do you do?"

"Say silly things, I guess."

"I must have missed that. Your saying something silly, I mean."

14

She laughed. Then she tried to check herself, and they both laughed.

"Well, Paolo, I would like you to make my little Sacha a magic room. Yes, I think I would like it very much."

"Is this real coffee?"

"Yes. Would you like some decaf?"

"Too late. Could we talk some more?"

Good. He too apprehended the spirit of the understanding between them.

"Tell me about Sacha."

She crooked her forefinger, pulling him up the stairs to the second floor where Sacha slept next to her room. Sacha's sandy hair had fallen over his one visible eye and when she brushed it back with her fingertips he opened the violet eye and she leaned over and kissed it shut.

When she glanced at Paolo he seemed beatified as if his eye too had been kissed.

Down in the big kitchen at the back of the house Natalya poured more coffee. "It's strange how we became a matrilinear family. We were standing by the window in Frankovsk—it's a Ukrainian city just north of the Carpathians—Irina and me, hand in hand, watching this spidery little German vehicle going from lamppost to lamppost putting up signs. You know, Do this! Do that! Report to, et cetera. It was still the honeymoon, I figured out later, the Nazis on their best behavior because not all the Ukrainians were unhappy to see them. So it was the last chance for Jews to get out. My father had a brother teaching at the Frunze in Moscow, a mathematician, and he was planning to smuggle us all back behind Red Army lines by the underground railway. So of course Irina and I wanted to know all about this railway, how many cars, how big was the locomotive, what mountains it went under, and so on. Our mother, Elena, is trying to laugh and put the best face on everything, but that's hardly the only thing she's doing. She's also arranging for me and Irina to go to Istanbul through Romania to friends of her family who'll arrange for us to sail to America to her sister Yekaterina

15

here in Baltimore. That's how we got here. Naturally she never tells my father until we're gone. We never saw them again. His head was spring-loaded, so I don't see how he could've survived those operatic thugs.

"She is my role model, she saw what had to be done and she did it, for us. You can live your whole life saying, I'm very forward-looking, I never look back, the past is past, everybody has ups and downs. But when the day comes the whole world turns to glass and you're slip-sliding off, then you have only one hope—namely somebody shows you how to be a detective."

"Why a detective?"

"Because there had been a grand theft of our innocence, a whodunnit—in our case, it was Irina's innocence and mine, and it was Papa who done it. Night after night, stinking of vodka and lies. Mama made us concubines. How could she not know? So when I say she is my role model, it's a very considered thing to say, because somehow the arrival of that army of undertakers inspired her—is that the right word, I wonder?—to a single act of heroism. This is what I had to reconstruct to be a psychiatrist, the chief of detectives, and it's why Sacha's here. In fact, it's why you're here. But why is Alice Miller important to you, Paolo?"

Paolo was a mile or two back in her narrative, trying to rappel off that glass. He had to shake himself to catch up.

"I had wonderful parents. They had been restaurateurs in Milan. Their place in Manhattan was really a salon where they fed artists and writers and actors, spiritually as much as anything. But I also knew a man in New York, handsome as you'll ever meet, who'd been betrayed, whipped till he turned feral. After I met him I began to see desperate kids everywhere I looked, kids who weren't in safe hands while the whole world is telling them how lucky they are. God, we wreck our kids!" He stood, unable to support such thoughts sitting.

Turned feral. Whipped till he turned feral. The precision of this phrasing made a danse macabre in her mind. She stood absentmindedly on tiptoe to touch his shoulder with her fingertips. Then, dismayed, she pressed on with her story, more to overlook her gesture than anything.

"Yekaterina was a lovely duck. That's what we called her, Ducky, because we were so sad when we got here, and she used to make us laugh by imitating animals. We'd squeal till we wet our pants when she did a mama duck waddling and quacking. It got to be sort of a code: whenever something was wrong, Ducky would make a hilarious face.

"Ducky had inherited a large amount of money from her husband. He made bedsprings. She loved art and would go to openings with us in tow. She was fruity and we loved her immensely. She'd say, May I introduce the Princess Irina and the Archduchess Natalya, and we'd play right along and curtsy. Ducky gave us wonderful educations. She was quite a bit older than Elena, ten or twelve years I think, but she took an active role in our lives—school, homework, friends, everything. She even took us to Orioles games and blatted huge Bronx cheers at the umpires. Oh, we loved her madly! We never spoke about Mama because we were insatiable readers and we sort of knew what had happened to her. At first we cried at night and when we did Ducky would take us into her bed and sing to us, and coo, Shush, shush, my little Frankovsk ducklings.

"Ducky was a super-patriot, so we assimilated much faster than many. Sometimes when she couldn't explain something she'd say, Well, it's the American way, my darlings. I don't know if it's rare in a woman but she wept during *God Bless America* and *The Star-Spangled Banner*.

"We both went to Hopkins. Irina is a botanist. She was always outgoing—her friends called her a firecracker. I was kind of introspective and dreamy. But it was funny, the jocks hit on me and the eggheads hit on her. Weird, huh?"

"Unh, unh, the jocks figured you were one of those rare brains who wouldn't dump on them, right?"

"Yes! It was a neat ticket for me—that way I didn't get painted into a corner, you know, stereotyped. Baltimore is probably one of the few cities in the world capable of producing Jewish jocks. But I went out with a lot of Christian boys, you know, from Saint Paul's and later on from Hopkins. Ducky's religion was iconoclasm, really, so we grew up agnostic, but Jung sort of baptized me. I don't know about Irina, except she told me out in Arkansas that she saw God in a dewdrop, and that's certainly more religion than I've ever had."

"Ducky died of leukemia the year before I graduated from medical school. We felt grateful she'd lived that long. We stayed together here on Charles Street for about a year before Irina decided to make a pilgrimage to Jim Morrison's grave in Père Lachaise Cemetery in Paris and said, Why don't you come, Natalya, you could visit Proust and Oscar Wilde. I enjoyed that we respected the differences between us. At least I thought we did. I couldn't go—I was doing my residency at Spring Grove. I got a few cards from around Europe, then nothing for five months. The next thing I heard she was living in a commune in Fort Smith, Arkansas, where they were growing herbs in concert with the devas and trying to market them. I can't imagine what the devas told them about all the marijuana they were growing. I stayed on here alone and worked at Hopkins. I think in Irina's mind I took Ducky's place. Otherwise she wouldn't have felt safe leaving.

"She called me one night to tell me she was having a baby. I guess she expected me to take the bait and ask her when she'd gotten married. I ask her, Are you happy? She says, It's just like you to ask something like that, Natalya! I say, Well, yes, I suppose it is. So, are you happy? I don't get an answer right away, which is not surprising because our conversations are always punctuated by long pauses.

"Then she says, He's a yahoo.

"I say, Who is?

"The baby's father.

"I see.

"You don't see, Natalya, you never see. He's a yahoo, you know—Yahoo, Mountain Dew!

"Well, aside from my not knowing Mountain Dew is a soft drink and never having heard the rebel yell—has anyone?—my idea of a yahoo was sort of literary, so it diverged pretty sharply from Irina's. I figured a yahoo—I guess I would have pronounced it yay-hoo—was a brutish person. But Irina seemed to mean a yokel, and in any case it didn't seem very flattering. But what really worried me was why she wanted to babble on about the baby's father when she hadn't bothered to mention him before.

"She said, If it's a girl I'm going to name her Guinevere, and if it's a boy I'll name him Lancelot or maybe Abercrombie. She was trying hard to be funny, but I was getting more and more worried by the minute. The old family scene. She could never get Ducky's goat, so she always went after mine. It ended up she named the boy Sacha, and that worried me too—as if she'd tried to step back on something firm by giving him an old-world name, not for him but for herself.

"Sacha must have been nine months old when I got a call from Sue Ellen Hendershott in the Fort Smith child protective services office. Sacha had a broken hip and was in a full body cast.

"A full body cast!

"Yes ma'am, Sue Ellen Hendershott says, he fell down some stairs and hurt himself.

"I'm a doctor, Miss Hendershott, maybe you better get to the point, I said.

"She says, Ma'am, the point is one of the doctors—the one your sister took the little fella to?—says the injuries are not consistent with your sister's account. She took the little boy to two emergency rooms before the one that treated him and when they started asking questions she just up and walked out with the boy. Seems like the third hospital—there was this nice doctor from Pakistan, y'know?—treated the little boy first and asked questions later. Well—the doctor from Pakistan?—he didn't like your sister's story, ma'am, so he reported it to the police and they reported it to us. The officer said the child's body was covered with bruises. You there, ma'am?

"I'm here, Miss Hendershott, I said.

"Well, we'd kinda like to know about your sister and her husband? We don't know who he is, and the living conditions where the child lives are pretty bad, ma'am. The neighbors are right upset, and there is some evidence of drug abuse. So we were wonderin' what you think we oughta do.

"Sue Ellen Hendershott sounded like a very decent, educated country girl. I liked the hypnotic interrogative way she talked and it sort of drew me to her, and to Sacha and Irina.

"I said, I'm coming down there right away. Could you give me an appointment?

"That would be right nice, Ma'am. We can talk about it.

"So I flew to Fort Smith and met Sue Ellen—she looked like a long-stemmed bluebell—and I liked her so much by the time I left I was saying dun't and wun't in her honor."

Paolo smiled broadly, enjoying the wry disposition of Natalya's mind and her ability to recall Sue Ellen's speech.

"I was packing when Irina called and said she was in trouble and could I come. I said, I'm coming."

"Little Tut in his mummy case is what he looked like, and from the moment he saw me he kept following me with his eyes. If I left the room and returned his eyes would be right on me as if I hadn't gone. I knew from the start I wasn't there to see Irina or Sue Ellen, I was there to see Sacha.

"Irina was freaked out. She seemed to be running the place, whatever it was, a big two-story green and white slambang of boards with a slew of falling-down corrugated metal sheds all around. Everything had gone to seed—a truck that looked like it'd been dropped off a building, the water pump groaned ominously, the vegetable garden looked like the devas went south. I couldn't figure out how the group could make enough money to feed themselves, and then it dawned on me they were dealing. Most of them were musicians, but it wasn't bluegrass they were devoted to.

"Buddy, Sacha's father—at least Irina thought he was the father—left on his Harley two days after Sacha was born. A nurse asked him if they'd decided on a name and he said, Ask his ole lady, and blew. Small loss. Irina doesn't even have a picture of him. She described him as sort of Confederate-looking and blond, so I figured he looked like one of those gut-punched stringbeans with a droopy moustache and hangdog slouch leering at pregnant teenagers down in Patterson Park.

"There was an old black lady who'd lived on the place when they bought it—I've always wondered where they got that money—and they let her stay in one of the shacks. She was worried about Sacha, I could tell. She would look at me and shake her head all the time, which was valuable information to me. I asked her about Buddy and she said, He be a good boy, daddy a preacher, mama a drugstore farm'cist lady, till he let those drum-bangin' so-called friends of his ovah ta Fawt Smith be tellin' him what to do allatime."

"That authentic?" Paolo asked.

"The accent? Oh no, I don't think so, but I do hear a lot of accents in my line of work and I like to amuse myself. Have you ever noticed folks from Bawl'mer say 'Danny Ocean, hunn' instead of 'down-to-the-ocean, honey'?"

"There's a certain way they use their sinuses to talk," Paolo said, "like when they say new it comes out something like nee-uu. It's quite a feat because they don't bunny-wrinkle their noses to do it."

"Do I do that?"

"Say new."

"I will not! I'll never say new again."

Paolo leaned back in her director's chair, put his hands behind his head, and closed his eyes to signal they'd digressed from her story.

"Irina didn't talk much the whole two weeks I was there. We took long walks in the meadow. It's very pretty country. I never mentioned Sacha's injuries. We took him into town about a week after I got there to have his cast checked and I guess he made a decision for his mother then and there. When the doctor finished with his cast he held his little arms out to me. After that it seemed I was carrying him around all the time and he would play with my hair and push it down over my eyes. Then one day we were walking high up in a meadow, just Irina and me, and she turned around to me and hugged me. I held her face in my hands like Ducky used to do when we were upset and I pressed my forehead up to hers and looked into her eyes.

"I'm sick, Natalya, she said, be his mother, be Sacha's mother, be his Ducky, I'll sign the papers. We sat down in the grass with the sun playing hide-and-seek in the clouds and braided wildflowers for a while and then we started to cry, and a week later I took him home with me."

Paolo patted himself. Natalya wondered if he smoked, but he was looking for a small sketchpad. Finding none, he got up and said, "I'll start tomorrow if that's okay with you." Tomorrow was Saturday and it became his habit to come Saturdays and work all day. Other days he'd call the night before. At first she left him keys to the double-door entry under a petunia marker stuck in a Virginia juniper planter. But within a few weeks he was coming by three or four evenings unannounced.

One of his obsessions led Paolo to Dominick Maggiore. It upset him to use tools and materials whose properties he didn't understand, and this same obsession drew Dom to Paolo. If Paolo was going to use a detail brush, for example, he wanted to know not only that it ought to be mink-bristled—but why mink bristles were best. He was loath to cede any secret to craft lore.

He figured he needed braces to reinforce the studs in Sacha's room, which he intended to bore through and in some cases interrupt. So he started calling metallurgists and getting secretarial brush-offs until Dom picked up his phone, as he always did, at the National Institute for Metallurgical Research.

"Steel," Dom said.

"Yes, but there's steel and there's steel—I know it sounds crazy, Dr. Maggiore, but I have to have just the right thing because this is a magical room and...."

Dom looked at the phone quizzically and then put it back to his ear. This is the best conversation I've had in years, he thought. "You're right, Mr. Maio. In fact, in view of what you say, steel might not even be the right answer. I better see the room."

Passion for content joined them.

22

"Listen, Ducky," Paolo told her that evening, "I'm stuck about how to brace the studs. So tomorrow a metallurgist is coming to advise us."

"A metallurgist?"

"I think he's a fellow zany."

"Do you always do this?"

Paolo waited for exposition. He knew it wasn't in Natalya's nature to even wonder what this fellow zany might cost and he hadn't bothered to tell her Dr. Maggiore had volunteered.

"Yes."

"And does it always work out?"

"One way or another, Natalya."

"This sounds like dialogue I have with patients."

Paolo looked stung, so Natalya murmured musically and said, "Oh you!"

"Paolo, I think our fellow zany is here," she called up the stairs next day. Paolo articulated himself down the stairs in the manner of the futurist Severini's paintings, his coveralls loud with tools.

"Domenico, I'm Paolo, and this is Natalya. Sacha is preoccupied."

The newcomer might be grasping her shoulders, so firmly his gravity held. His amber eyes embraced Paolo with palpable goodwill. When he turned them to Natalya she found in them something she could define later only as solace. In this pivotal instant she learned that Paolo, far from being indiscriminately friendly as she feared, allowed himself all the time he needed to consider a new persona. He was not to be had cheaply. His approval meant something.

Dominick Maggiore, she saw, was one of those men whose eyes linger without disquieting—gracing rather than importuning. His carved mouth looked good-humored, not humorous like hers. A Roman proconsul, she decided, judicious, fair, but not readily accessible. Paolo on the other hand was a Lombard prince, not destined like an older brother to inherit, but happily given purview of the arts.

Such wispy reveries Natalya entertained as they climbed

up to Sacha's room—that is, his former room, for he was now removed down the hall to Ducky's bedroom, overlooking the hidden garden at the back.

To her dismay, she saw that Paolo had already gutted the room so that its laths and studs stood bare.

"I'm going to transform the ceiling into a domed vault," he was saying. "I wish I could raise it, but a second floor ceiling is a bit much to raise if you intend to use the room above. I'd like to cut a skylight in the ceiling upstairs, then echo it with another down here, but that stands in the way of another plan I have for this ceiling. I don't know quite how yet, but I did this in New York once for a friend, so I know I can figure it out. The idea is it will present the night sky—so Sacha can sleep under the heavens as the Medicis loved to do." He let that sink in.

And was rewarded: "If you have the heavens on your mind the world needn't be such a hellish place," Dom confided to the room itself.

"I have to steal about two feet from the walls, so it's a good thing it's a big room. I want to fill the walls with secret caches, you see—an aquarium, a terrarium—and inside these walls," he gestured to his right, "I'd like to install HO gauge trains, with countryside and villages."

"Lombardy?" Natalya asked. But she was fixed on Dom's having failed to ask how any of this would be done: not a querulous, self-important man, this fellow zany.

"I'll put secret compartments in the floor too, but I'm not sure what kind of handles to use."

"Recessed brass ring-pulls perhaps," Dom said. He read Paolo's expression finely: the artist was delighted but he didn't get it, so Dom made a flat loop with his left forefinger and thumb and pried it up with his right forefinger. Paolo laughed.

"Everything has to be wired. Fortunately the house is already 220 volts. The sashes I'll take out and put in a wall-to-wall bow window with a seat. I haven't discussed this with Natalya, but I'm kind of worried the bow window will alter the facade in some moogy way."

"Moogy?" Natalya said, "as in Moog synthesizer?"

"Yeah, muzzy," Paolo said.

She was about to chuckle when she saw Dom nodding as if he knew just what Paolo meant. "Lombard strips," he said, aiming a sly smile at Paolo, "they just might give the bow window a rather considered elegance."

"Postmodern nostalgic," Paolo said, catching on.

Natalya was so pleased her toes tingled. She had no idea what Lombard strips were but admired the giftedness of Dom's response: to salute Paolo's heritage while making a helpful suggestion.

By the time he'd described a Lombard strip—faux pilasters joined at the top by little arches—she and Paolo were fanatic partisans. The three of them were as exhilarated by what they were discovering about each other as they were about the room. "What do you think about the vault, Domenico?" He had expected Dom to pass on the merit of the idea.

"Well, enlarging the window could help with the vault." He could not yet bring himself to say, Paolo, but he enjoyed being called Domenico. "We could hoist the entire night sky up from the street through the hole before you install the new window. The strips of course can come any time."

He had Paolo's full attention. Paolo had intended to do it all in place with plaster, as he had in Matt Pieto's apartment in New York.

"The boatyards are hurting for business. If we can get the measurements down to where we know we need the holes for the major stars to be illuminated, we can have a yard fabricate two fiberglass semi-domes. Then we rig block and tackle on the roof and we hoist them and set them down on a fairly shallow cantilever."

"Magnifico!"

"Then you can paint the night sky, or if you prefer, you can paint it before we raise it."

"Phosphorescent paint, I'll use phosphorescent paint."

"I can pre-wire the halves of the dome so all we have to do is wire them into the house circuitry. Actually, I don't think the vault necessarily precludes the double skylight. The hemispheres can be made retractable. The eye opens and shuts."

"Yeah, but we've got a door on one side and a window on the other," Paolo fretted.

"Sure, but all you've got is walls right and left, right? We'll have to poke around, see what's what."

"You'll help, Domenico?"

"Yeah, I'd like to."

Natalya was wondering whether to express her childish glee when she realized she already had, clasping her hands as when Ducky unwrapped some wondrous gift. Pleasure opened Paolo's face.

"I'll have to study the stars," he said. "You know, figure out which ones to fire at this latitude."

"Latitude and season," Dom said. "Polaris, Deneb, Arcturus for sure. Fact is, you could pick a night. Sacha's birth night maybe."

"You know the stars?"

"I navigate. I have a boat." He walked along the north wall of the room touching the lath. "Maybe we could recess a diorama of the ancient Nile, you know, through a peephole. Depends on how much top room we need to retract the vault. I'm sort of an amateur Egyptologist."

"Listen—about the braces, Domenico, what do you think?"

"I think we really need steel fascia with oculuses and rectangles for viewing. See, if you think about it, the studs have to go to make room to retract the vault, but you still want to recess various and sundry delights in the wall."

"Steel walls?"

"Galvanized, yeah. There are options. Gotta think about it. Weight's a factor. I can fabricate what we need. I have a little workshop in an alley on The Hill."

"What do you make?"

"Tangs and swages mostly. When I get ambitious I do turnbuckles and blocks."

Paolo loved the arcane nomenclature.

"Tangs fix a boat's rigging to its hull, to coaming or bulkheads. They get a lot of stress and I got tired of paying the yard for bum metal from Taiwan. Swages have eyes in them and you use them and turnbuckles to adjust the tension of the rigging. Lots of stress and fatigue."

"What's rigging?" Paolo asked.

"Oh. Rigging is what holds the mast up and the mast is what you set the sails on." Dom put some wired silver glasses on to examine the studs, then pocketed them and looked at Paolo.

"What's your boat's name?" Paolo asked. Dom turned to Natalya with the answer. *"Nefertiti."*

"The exquisite consort of the heretic pharaoh Akhenaton," she said.

"Some call her the most beautiful woman in all history," Paolo said.

"Yes, because of an artist like you," Dom said.

How pleasant this naive communion is, Natalya thought, considering all the machismo she'd sloughed to help men get at their diseases. Women too. "I'm going to fix lunch," she said to break her spell. Again Dom surprised them.

"Have you started it yet?"

"No."

"Well, there's this great market in Baltimore, Grimaldi's. Let me run out for some things and I'll fix us a little colazione." He made a ringed perfecto of forefinger and thumb.

She ought to have protested—she was the host. But she wanted to see Dom Maggiore working in her kitchen.

"That would be wonderful, Domenico," she said. "I'll go open a bottle of Valpolicella."

When he returned Dom put on Natalya's dancing dolphins apron and whipped up veal piccata with capers and thin lemon slices, vermicelli and tossed salad. As they sat down they found without mentioning it that they were at best abstemious drinkers, and Natalya put out a bottle of sparkling cider to keep their repast festive. Dom raised opened palms and said, "Let us keep the feast."

"Alleluia," Paolo said.

It was the first day of a tradition—soon Dom, a talented Sicilian chef, took it on himself to serve up the tomatoless dishes of Lombardy and Tuscany in Paolo's honor. But it was

Sacha who drew Dom into the magicians' circle. The boy, from that day, kept handing him his dearest objects—Babar the empathic pachyderm, his chewable books, his biscuits, his green plastic telephone—and Dom gravely examined each gift, discussing their work with Babar, tasting a book, sampling a biscuit, making a telephone call to Sacha, while Sacha's long violet eyes glowed appreciatively. Dom would wrap a strand of vermicelli around his finger and vacuum it into his mouth, then he would wind a strand around Sacha's finger and nod approvingly when the boy popped it into his own mouth. The boy loved to ride on Paolo's shoulders, was content to watch him for long periods in silence, and awarded him gleeful smiles—but the serious commerce between Dom and Sacha informed Natalya and Paolo that the sweetness of the man's nature was evident to the child.

"He needs us," Natalya said when Dom left that first day.

"We need him," Paolo replied, picking Sacha up high over his head, "right, Sacha, our little catalyst?" Then, following his nature, he mused that catalysts are something our new friend Dom Maggiore knows all about.

They worked rhythmically. Two or three nights a week Dom drove the fifty minutes it took him to get from his Dupont Circle apartment in Washington to Charles Street in Baltimore. He usually worked in Sacha's room from seven to ten. Paolo would leave him notes about what he'd done during the day. Dom concentrated first on measurements, then he drew wiring diagrams.

He was shyer with children than with adults, something that interested Natalya. He would gaze on the sleeping Sacha each night before leaving, and more often than not Sacha would open an eye and smile the most trusting smile she had ever seen. It seemed to her that not even she was granted such benedictions. On Saturdays the men worked together while Sacha accompanied Natalya on her errands.

It soon became their habit—when weather allowed—to rendezvous in Deale on Sundays, the four of them, and to sail aboard *Nefertiti*. Natalya knew but wouldn't say that Paolo and Dom had begun sailing together some afternoons and evenings. Nor did she tell them that one of her favorite reveries was of the two men ghosting before a smoky sun in the black boat. This, she knew, conformed to Jung's archetypal notions, but, experienced as she was, she could not crack its code, all her efforts striking her as obvious, therefore suspect. Solar boat, journey to the nether world, gods accompanying a dead pharaoh—the whole Wallis Budge lexicon. Nothing clicked as the vision pervaded her. But it made her feel powerful, as if she were the very air in *Nefertiti*'s sails or even the sun that gives rise to wind. And in this last sensibility she was not far from the mark, for day-sailing though they all were, she, Sacha and Alice Miller's room were most certainly *Nefertiti*'s navigational stars—they and the captain's hidden purpose in life, his predicament.

Dom so unobtrusively imparted the commands and idiom of sailing to Paolo and Natalya that they began to style their own. For example, when they had cleared the dock and fairway, and were ready to transit from engine to wind, one of them, instead of saying, Cut the engine, would say, Blessed moment, because that is how Dom had described the snuffing of the diesel, the uncrumpling whumph of the canvas and shush of water at the bow. Paolo shorthanded this signal to making the sign of the cross in the air, a benediction of silence, and Natalya made it clear she much preferred it to Dom's thumb-across-the-throat.

Before she heard of Vince Grifaci, that is.

She relished their interest in each other's work, mindful always that Paolo had been the catalyst. One Saturday, waiting for them to arrive—it would be Paolo in white coveralls with tools and buckets, Dom with bags of food and gadgets—she felt loquacious, and she yakked unconscionably at the usually reserved Sacha, thinking, Yes, Dr. Yasdarov, you talk for a living and, lucky you, you have three males who like to listen. Hey Natalya, give yourself a break, you also listen for a living.

"So we've got four listeners here, Sacha!" Sacha liked this remark, beaming a big Da and dumping a spoonful of pear mash on his head. "Da?" she said. No daddy around, it must be Russian. That's funny, she mused, I must talk more Russian to Sacha than I think. "Da," she affirmed.

Once the work had begun she executed her mission for the day. "Paolo, how did you come by your infinite curiosity?"

Dom offered up one of those this-is-going-to-be-good looks.

"It started with a careful study of the wood grain in my crib."

"I think his mother had curious milk," Dom said.

"I wish I remembered," Paolo said.

"Oh you!" Natalya pushed him playfully, "I bet you do."

"I don't see how you could be an artist and not want to know about wood, paint, chemicals—the whole nine yards," Paolo said. "By the way, do you know where that expression comes from? Concrete mixers carry nine cubic yards. I don't know, when I think about it, it's very American: Americans are fixers, handymen. When a German tank conked out they sat and waited for the mechanic. The Americans jury-rigged her and cranked her over."

"Hear that?" Dom said, "he's a sailor now. Sailors jury-rig everything, even broken hearts."

"I heard jury-rig and a great deal besides," Natalya started, "so much, I don't know where to start. I heard him call the tank her, for one thing."

"Yes, he cranked her over," Dom said.

"And you with your jury-rigged broken hearts, how do you jury-rig a broken heart?" Paolo asked.

Sadness ambushed him midway to finding an answer. The moment stood in stasis as the three of them wrestled with the phrase. Then Dom took it as duty to restore their pleasure. "I guess the only people who really don't interest me are the incurious."

"You're the inheritor of the alchemical tradition," Paolo said. "You know, dross to gold. Except on a mystical plane that's not what they were talking about at all."

"What then?" Dom asked.

"What Natalya does—taking the human spirit by the hand and helping it up the stairs."

"Do I do that?"

"I hope you do."

"I think you must," Dom said.

"What do you do, Domenico?" Paolo asked.

"Confront and clarify."

"How?"

Dom searched their eyes for seriousness. He searched so long and so intently that Paolo was about to forgive the burden when Natalya shook her head at him, warning him to wait. "I reached a certain point as a student," Dom began, "where I felt I was remembering everything I needed to know. I felt like that remembering got me through the tough parts. But it was so eerie I repressed the idea. Then when I'd get stumped at NASA years later, I recalled that feeling and I started breaking through again. But you can forget past-life regression because we were up on the cutting edge."

"Parallel times," Natalya thought aloud.

This elicited from Dom a kind of groping look, dimly lit by remembrance.

Ten on the Richter Scale, Paolo thought.

"This is going to be a very magical room," Natalya said. "All our thoughts, all we've shared, is going to be in this room with Sacha."

They sat in the center of their thoughts until Dom said, "I thought magic thinking was a no-no among shrinks."

"They wouldn't have had to invent the phrase if it had no validity," she said. "Besides I'm a fink shrink. Some like to pop clients' balloons, I like to pop the industry's balloons. I snitch to clients."

"That's the stuff, Yasdarov!" Paolo yelled down from the ceiling where he was hole-sawing beams. "You've got the damndest library I ever saw. I think what you are is an explorer."

Paolo Magus—you never know what juxtaposition of events he's going to engineer, but you can be sure he's not going to just string them together. Well, he's a painter, she thought, painters push paint. And while she shaped this reflection she watched Dom's lips form but withhold the word explorer. Living with you two is like breaking through with a client eight hours a day. She took note of her words, living with, and as usual checked her impulse to voice the thought, for fear of changing everything that was changing her. The image of three babes at a wolf's teats came to her fertile mind. Then four.

What should a woman dare, watching these men wholly intent on the life of her child? She would dare nothing, spoil nothing. Some things are better than carnal love—or at least it should be so to anyone who aspires to anything like wisdom. These are scarred men healing, like myself. We are good for each other, she thought, rising to make coffee.

When she returned she stood at the gutted opening of what would be Sacha's room with a tray of heirloom silver and coffee, watching her unexpected friends. Paolo sat in a jumble of his long, crossed legs and tools, drafting on his sketchpad, Dom knelt in a corner—rapt, as if in an Islamic prayer niche—wiring a transformer. They reminded her of Frankovsk Hasidim davening.

Can the goyim accept you as an equal, even when they love you? Wretched thought. Back, ethnicity! She felt like Van Helsing showing Dracula the cross. These men were her friends, why should love intrude? Better lack than spoil this exquisite thing. Dom looked up and smiled, shy, uncertain at being observed. What happens in that excellent man's mind? Seven years, he'd told her, he'd been in therapy. With a Jungian I hope, she'd thought, so rich the man's secret life. That was clear, he was so other-directed he'd need a therapist who wouldn't disparage—what? His illusions? A therapist who wouldn't call them illusions—that's it. And Paolo, he is a demi-god. Where are his flaws? That he couldn't love, connect? Perhaps. But what is all this, if not love? To love a god is unprofitable; to love a man who is not there, unwise. Still, she profits from Paolo, and Dom is here often and devotedly. No, sensual love is not everything. Nor are its risks invariably worth taking, even if you are still young and needy. Can't wisdom ever belong to the young?

32

"Russian gasoline, gentlemen," she said, holding out the tray.

"I thought that meant vodka," Paolo said.

"Not if you're a Jewish Russky."

Strained thoughtfulness darkened Dom's face. The intimation of apartness troubles him, she thought. She set her tray on the floor between them and touched his shoulder fleetingly. He smiled to himself and brightened. She felt rewarded for her insight. Presence, there is a presence among us. Refrain, Natalya, quell your compulsion to define. What you see is what you get. Friendship is worth more than affairs—let time sort it out.

She sat cross-legged. Did they see her womanliness? Surely Paolo savored her fluid hands, the echo of the Bolshoi in her shadowed calves. Had she now two brothers, three sons, pro bono clients? Paolo slipped off her shoes and laid his sketchpad on her feet. "It's the sliding doors," he said. This casualness in so intimate a maneuver amused her, pleased her. Signifying? I don't care, she thought. Nowhere in her short eventful life—from smirking Red apparatchiks to women-loathing Freudians—had she encountered respite. Yet here was respite, in the company of free, supportive men. Whatever else is going on here, or not going on here, don't forget that, Dr. Yasdarov. If these guys want something from you, it's not intruding, and they are not poker players. Waking in copses of their beings probably—but not frightened, just stirring meditatively.

She liked this picture.

Dom began explaining the transformer. Jeez, he's explaining mechanics to a woman as if she cared. Did she say Jeez? Jewess, the goyim are getting you. But Jesus was a Jew. She giggled.

Dom's right eyebrow arched. "It's funny," he said. "I mean this is so primitive, twenty years from now it'll look like a Model T."

Never missed a beat. I do like this man. "Are you always so absorbed in what you do?"

Paolo took interest.

"Yes," replied Dom.

"And so are you, I see, Dr. Yasdarov," Paolo said.

She was about to giggle again when it occurred to her she didn't even know she knew how to giggle until she met these men. Had she giggled as a child? She thought not. Then she giggled again.

"That's how I like to paint women," Paolo continued.

"Absorbed?"

He nodded.

"Not men?"

"I'd like to paint Domenico."

Dom gave him a thoughtful look.

"Well, that's a cop-out, but I'll let you get away with it," she said. "Why are you Paolo—and not Paul?"

"We always spoke Italian when I was growing up, so by the time I went to Saint John's everybody knew me as Paolo. Then I went to Florence to study and I lived with my parents up in the hills. Well, actually I lived in the Uffizi, to tell you the truth. North Italians don't Americanize with the vengefulness of the Sicilians. The Sicilians are passionate Americans."

"North Italians don't do anything with the vengefulness of the Sicilians, except paint," Dom said rather dourly.

"I mean, the Sicilians were just so glad to get here, to become Americans."

"You're not?" Dom asked.

"Sure I am, but I still like to use Paolo. It sounds better than Paul in any language."

"So do I," Natalya said.

"Yeah, I do too, in spite of his Lombard condescension to Siciliani," Dom said.

"I wasn't condescending. Some of my best friends are Sicilian: Matt Pieto, Dom Maggiore...."

"Ahma gonna changa you face, you Lombard snob!" Dom shoved Paolo over, both of them laughing. I bet that's the first time in his life Dom has ever rough-housed like that, she thought.

"Maggiore's a northern name, Dom, so how're you Sicilian?"

"Piemonte actually, around Turino. A lot of North Italian families moved to Sicily as Victor Emmanuel's bureaucrats. Maggiores from Piemonte, uGucciones from Firenze and Roma, lots of them. Must've been some king! Imagine moving from

Firenze to Misilmeri? But they soon got as poor as the rest of the rock farmers, and so they ended up on Ellis Island."

"With the Mafia?" Natalya asked.

"What Mafia?"

Paolo laughed. "The Americans needed a mafia, you know, to replace the cowboys and the cavalry. Hollywood needed a mafia. Now Hollywood tells the Italians all about it."

But Paolo's joviality soured when his mind sent north to Matt, grandson of two great Mafia families, his old and dear college friend. Matt would love what they were doing in this room. He should call him and tell him.

"I find the whole idea of being Sicilian in the midst of the Mafia comforting," said Natalya. "A whole lot more than being a Jew in the midst of Ukrainians and storm troopers."

Dom stuck out his arms, laced his fingers and stretched them backwards, his face impassive. He started to speak, then stopped like a chagrined stammerer.

"Parlatti," Paolo urged.

The sound of Italian jolted Dom. "Ever hear of Vince Grifaci?"

Paolo combed back his hair with Botticelli fingers. He nodded without looking at Dom. The dozens of meals Matt and his grandfathers had eaten in Nicola and Ariella Maio's place, and the dozens of meals he'd eaten at Gus Pieto's and John Altobene's, had familiarized Paolo with the entire New York Mafia genealogy.

"Staten Island," he said.

"Charlie Luciano's goombah. My father Tony was a button. He bought it in Union City. Big John Altobene put a hit out on him."

Natalya saw Paolo stiffen, hold his breath and shut his eyes. His mouth tightened his face into a skull. She guessed the reason. She registered Dom's seeming indifference to Paolo's familiarity with the Mafia. Dom was now talking to himself.

"I lived with my mother, Sorella, near Vince's. It was no big deal—my father, Tony, was never home. One day, Sorella—she took the ferry over to Manhattan to her job and never came back. When I think about it, it's weird, because I never called her office. I think I just knew. I was eleven. I went to school, I came home, I cleaned the house, I studied, I figured something would happen. Vince came by after about ten days maybe. I met him at the door with the vacuum cleaner.

"He said, So, kid, you helping your mother?

"She's gone.

"Yeah? Where'd she go?

"I dunno, I said. I was trying not to cry—feeling like my face is bursting. Vince came in and started to walk around, opening drawers and closets. Then he sat down in the living room in kind of a heap.

"Dom, get a beer for you Uncle Vince.

"I brought him a Rupert's from the fridge, which was by now almost empty. And he said, So, Dom, you like you Uncle Vince? I nodded my head because I did. He said, That's good, kid, because you and me, we got a little work to do.

"It turned out we had a lot of work to do—bringing me up. Angelena and Vince were good to me, kind, but they didn't love me. You feel those things. They treated me as well as they treated Tommy, their son, who was thirteen—better really, because they saw I was a good student and they sent me to good schools. Tommy—he just wanted to hang out, like my father, like his father when you think about it. We're friends still. Vince sent me to Hopkins. I still remember peeling off his crisp green bills to the bursar." Dom fell silent.

Paolo's eyes were still closed, his mouth set.

Natalya wondered how to get Dom to continue.

Then Dom said, "I'd never go back to New York. Give me Sicilians my age, I'll give you ghosts." Silence enfolded him again.

"Vince and Angelena. Do you see them now?" Natalya asked.

"She's dead. Vince I see, I write, he calls. Last year he called and said, Dr. Maggiore, this is you Uncle Vince. Listen, we got a wedding here. Josephine—remember you cousin Josephine? She wasn't my cousin, but I did remember her fondly.

"I said, I'm glad she found a good man, Uncle Vince.

"Dom, he's good and stupid. Listen, we gotta have some class at this wedding. You gonna come for you Uncle Vince—okay, kid?

"That kind of thing. He's proud of me, but I'm not his son."

Altobenes and Pietos swarmed Paolo's mind, but he found no way, not here, not now, to explain. He settled for "I understand."

What? she thought. What did you understand? What is a button? Her throat tightened on Dom's sorrow, so ineffable, and Paolo's response, empathic yet guarded. Surely his grief for the loss of his mother could not still be so livid. My new friends are mafiosi—not in practice, but emotionally. She'd strayed where the mind slowed. It took her whole minutes to guess that Dom, reticent son of violence, told this story not of his own need, but because he assumed that her remark about the apartness of Frankovsk's Jews had risen from a tarn of remembered pain and called out for as much fellow feeling as he could handle.

"Luciano liked Jews. His unofficial consiglieri was Meyer Lansky."

"This is a compliment maybe?" she asked.

Flustered, Dom said, "No, Natalya, it's interesting, is all."

"So can I be our consiglieri?"

Dom looked like the kid with a violin case who was being good-naturedly jostled by a jock. But he rose to the occasion. "Dominus vobiscum, spiritu et sancti," he said, making a cross in the air. "Now you're an honorary mafioso." But when he glanced at Paolo he saw that Paolo was not amused.

"Really?" Natalya said, "not just a youngish woman in black?"

"Heavy, Natalya, heavy." Paolo was dour.

Heavy, yes, they'd gotten into something heavy. Dom looked worried. She had strayed into the dark. The door could not be closed.

But she tried. "Does this mean I'm a Christian now?"

"I would like whatever you were," Dom said, avoiding her gaze.

"Now that's worthy of a papal nuncio," Paolo said. "If some nuncio had said that to Elizabeth, England would still be Catholic."

I believe you, sincere soul, Natalya thought, as unable to look at Dom as he'd been unable to look at her.

Love? Paolo asked himself. I love them both. Would I, if they were in love with each other? I hope so.

Paolo's unsettled, she thought. Let it be so, she hoped. Let it not be so, she hoped. Please, you damned man-woman thing, don't break this circle, our enchantment.

It didn't break. A squall had passed through, knocking them about, and when the sun returned it shone brightly on an altered and disarrayed place: Dom's disclosure, Paolo's queer response. They struggled like docked fish to get back to their deeps. These men both had dark roots and hers had surfaced and scorched.

Good time for chores. She peeked into Ducky's room. Sacha was nattering to the learned Babar. As always when he saw her he lifted up his arms to be carried. She changed him and carried him into his former room with his playpen. In a minute or two Dom was handing Sacha instruments and seriously discussing them, and he was waving up at Paolo on his ladder. She returned to Ducky's room and began straightening up.

You like Paolo and Dom, don't you, Ducky?

Do you, duckling?

Oh yes—very, very much. A metallurgist so skilled his work is secret—does he work on invisible airplanes?—educated by a Vince Grifaci, a gangster. And an artist trained in Florence who knows who Vince Grifaci is. Dr. Yasdarov, what a marvelous path you walk. I wouldn't trade this to be director of the Menninger.

"I think this room needs a little hidden recognition of Alice Miller," she said when she returned.

"Why? Is she dead?" Dom asked.

"Immortal," Paolo said. Natalya rocked his bony knee gratefully. "She has a great face," he continued, "a lot like Doris Lessing's."

"What an eye, Paolo!" she said. Ducky had been an ardent admirer of the English Sufi.

"My secret fantasy is to be a casting director," he told Dom. "What's yours?"

"To be an extraterrestrial."

38

Paolo seemed to lose interest, or at least nothing further was heard from on high. But when she looked up she saw him considering Dom through the braces of the ladder.

In the thickening silence, with Dom looking as if he were summoning the kundalini, Natalya's favorite psychiatric sin beset her—the inspired intervention: "Did you ever read Lessing's *Briefing for a Descent Into Hell?*"

"I will," Dom said, jotting the title in his Naval Institute daybook. When he does read it, weeks later—considering the protagonist whose veil of amnesia keeps lifting and fluttering down again, tormenting him with unacceptable visions of his purpose on earth—Dom wonders if he ought ever to see his new friends again.

Downstairs in the kitchen puttering, she asks herself, Am I the woman of their lives? She smiles. No, I am the women in their lives. She shivers with a recognition: I can't love two men, can I? I'd rather they have each other's affection than one of them have me. Lovely bind. Well, that's the life of an empath. And anyway, I have Sacha.

"Sacha is Sandro, Alessandro in Italian," Paolo said when she returned, as if their thoughts married and could be picked up at places downstream and mused over privately. Her nipples poked her shirt and she drew in her chest to reclaim privacy. Respite advanced to communion. What was possible? Everything. I should be scared, but I'm not.

I want to ask you one thing, Natalya, she said to the mirror in her dressing cove one morning, before dressing Sacha, before her housekeeper Mrs. Bedenbaugh arrived: Who do you look like?

She smoothed her eyebrows with her pinky. No, that's not what I want to ask. Danielle Darrieux. Hmmm, not bad. Yes, I think so, I have the nose, the heartbreaking nose. Do they pine? That's what I want to ask. Do they pine? What a queer question. Dom pines, Paolo probably not. I don't think he pines for you, Natalya. Do you pine, Natalya?

My father said, My offspring should be a rabbi, but God has cursed me with women. That's what he said. Cursed you with something far worse than women, Father. A rabbi? A tank commander is what I should have been, to chew you up in my tracks. Not once, not once did you say I was beautiful, Papa. Not once did you describe the man who might deserve me.

So listen Papa, I will describe him. His name is Paolo Maio. His name is Domenico Maggiore. Goyim, Papa! Yes, I'm here in America, in Yekaterina's house. I'm the mother of your favorite daughter's child. I studied harder than a rabbi, Papa. I'm a doctor, a psychiatrist. You would not even understand my question. I don't understand it, but I like it very much. She limned the lipstick at the corner of her mouth with a flourish and winked at her other gray eye. This is going to be a good day, Danielle.

What an angry son of a bitch! Paolo snapped his charcoal stick on his sketchpad as Willem de Kooning's savage renderings of women visited him unbidden. I wonder who screwed him around. No, I don't, I wouldn't want to paint her, once is enough.

Unlike many of his peers, Paolo was a classical draftsman. He regarded the formalist obsession with the medium as a deathward divorce, and standing in front of a Motherwell, had told Matt Pieto that a formalist's hell is an endless round of symposia in a Gothic cathedral. "You're a stinking academic!" Ragnar Halvorsen shouted at him in a Venice café one night. Ragnar, a blindered minimalist, thought Paolo's habit of working in abstract, semi-abstract and representational modes a peculiar anal retentiveness—particularly his passion for painting people he liked. Perhaps because he was not poor, perhaps because his work did sell, Paolo had always studied art, not art criticism, and pronunciamentos seemed as meritorious to him as desalting baccala.

Paolo hoisted his bed to the ceiling by a chain fall. His loft five blocks up South Broadway from the funky harbor in Fells Point echoed the tugs' eerie warnings. The bed's finished white underside harbored two rectangles of swiveling high-intensity lamps so that, lit aloft, it resembled various renderings of UFOs. It was emblematic of his sleeping habits—sleep being an alien intruder. He catnapped around the clock, often lying down wherever his work was, so as to remain under its influence. The loft—1,700 square feet and 27 feet high—reflected his restless experimentation with materials. Paolo regarded hardware stores as neglected sculpture courts. Dom once suggested he roller-skate between his various tasks: "I saw that French movie, too," Paolo said, laughing.

Probably what drew the men to each other at first was their pleasure in each other's energy: Paolo's loft and Dom's boat were intense gestures of resolve. Instinctively they each respected another man who'd spend hour after hour alone crafting such a statement. In Dom it might signal to a woman his preference for the inanimate. In Paolo the signal was more likely that creativity would always come first.

Natalya knew *Nefertiti* but not Paolo's loft. *Nefertiti* signaled only to her heart—what, she would not have been able to say. An elegant loneliness perhaps. The loft she imagined Spartan, Milano-modern. Its genius would have surprised her only in that she would have thought it something Paolo would make for others, not himself. That he'd done it for himself she might have found somehow reassuring.

Dom's theory about why Paolo had not shown her his loft was that he feared the numerous nude studies might unnerve her. But they could have been put away easily. The only separate room Paolo had, besides the partitioned bathroom, was a huge storeroom where his framed work, covered in glassine, hung in hundreds of fish-line cradles from ceiling tracks.

The studio's twenty-six-by-seventeen-foot domed Lexan skylight was in fact a planetarium. He'd kept the I-beams in place to use as hoist fulcrums. Twenty-five feet below was a modeling dais, but on many nights Paolo put a table and telescope on it and hoisted himself up to his little planetarium—using a heavy-purchase block and tackle that delighted Dom when he saw it.

Everything was engineering white, except the bleached floors, offending some of his artist friends who saw in muted white a better work environment. Paolo said he liked the challenge of angling lights against the remorselessness of the engineering white. It's what he thought an artist ought to say. His real reason was he liked the way it remembered and dehisced the *bois de rose* neon with which he'd lined the right angles of the loft. He'd nearly driven neon fabricator Myron Szarek around another kind of bend trying to arrive at the right hue. It was no good at all for work, of course, but it was meditative. He had, as well, lined all the vertical and horizontal corners of his closets with white neon that tripped on when the sliding doors were breached. Dom was predictably crazy in love with the place, and one of Paolo's more whimsical regrets soon became that everything he had done mechanically Dom would have done electronically.

One of Paolo's architectural obsessions—he associated it with the voids and vortices of the female form—was the incredible amount of space between beams and studs. It waited on his tongue to be asked that probably the most masculine thing he'd ever done was to fill these spaces. Obscenely? he sometimes wondered.

In no fewer than sixteen places in his immense floor he'd cut out the planking and replaced it with thick Lucite slabs incised with finger holes. Lighting was tripped when the hinged slabs were lifted. Into these cubbies Paolo stuffed the impedimenta of his life so that walking across Paolo's floor was rather like ice-skating over collages. Between twelve wall studs he installed small illumined sculptures, his oiled tools, and a few paintings.

In a vignette of their friendship it amused Paolo to see Dom fingering the corners of these interstices.

"You're wondering about insulation?"

Dom turned and smiled.

"Nowadays it's possible to use much thinner materials, like a plastic sheath. The Swedes are always producing some new insulator."

"Is that what you used?"

"Ummm, foamboard with a vapor barrier—and global warming."

"Where did you buy the latter?"

"In the cuckoo shop upstairs." He pointed to his head.

"The metallurgical lab at Cornell took a look years ago at some nickel filings recovered from a supposed site of a UFO crash in Cherry Valley, New York, and determined that the density was unlike anything on earth. That was no cuckoo shop."

Paolo stood becalmed in a regatta of six easels on which he had drawn Dom from memory. It was his habit to draw simultaneously, to come to terms in this way with how he experienced a person. He would pace from one brush stroke to another so that the last or next-to-last drawing often seemed the right one, but not always.

But now as he did this Natalya took shape.

Would she? Perhaps Natalya would pose nude for him—but sketching her in his mind, as he did often, convinced him afresh that he couldn't do it. It wasn't seemly.

How huge Ragnar would roar at that! But then Vikings had long before ceded the seemly to the Italians. So erotic he found every nuance and shade of her that it would shatter their triadic friendship, the shards would wound them, and they would back away from each other to heal. An artist should know when not to paint.

He left his six metallurgists and walked over to a great, yawing mural of whales breaching a moonlit sea. He chuckled to think of the Mexican Siqueiros saying muralism is the only path. Sure, for a Mexican leftist named Siqueiros. Siqueiros could have spit the dictum in his face and Paolo would have approved the invective without giving the message a thought. Not that he was always impassive. He had, for example, a quarrel with abstract expressionists, the boodle of whom he thought vulgarly confessional.

If Natalya Yasdarov struck him as his anima encountered, he'd keep it to himself for the sake of something rarer. A thought came now to lighten his sad reverence: perhaps the Bellinis and dear Sandro Botticelli, like Yeats suffering lust in old age, benefited greatly from restraint. Or call it constraint if you like: a court artist could not, prudently or otherwise, young or old, court a Medici contessa and be left free to immortalize her. Rationalizing piffle, Maio. But these introspections relieved him. He well understood what makes Van Goghs mad: their minds are completely uninsulated from the impressions that roar down upon them. They have no filters; they take everything in. That is why he worked with six easels and took long meditative walks between them, so as not to be sucked into one of them and vanish. Dr. Yasdarov would like to hear this, Maio—but, upon reflection, she too might prefer restraint. We are conspirators, he thought, and I like our conspiracy very much.

Having by now read three Alice Miller books, deeply moved, Dom wondered why Paolo, a man who'd been greatly loved and nurtured by gentle parents, had diverted the flow of his life to making this room for someone else's child. Was it a kind of tribute to Nicolo and Ariella, his parents? A brilliant regression from what he'd initiated in his workplace? Both?

For some reason, maybe no reason, neither Natalya nor Paolo had told him the answer: Matt Pieto's other good friend, Billy, the boy whipped feral, Matt's gift to his grandfather John Altobene, his grandfather's upper hand, La Famiglia's most feared assassin. Paolo had not told Natalya any more than he had on their first encounter. He had not told Matt how Billy Salviati haunted him. He could not tell anyone until he himself understood.

Because now Paolo would have to say, I looked in his face and I saw Jesus Christ.

Dom's own reason for doing this work was at first Paolo, whom he liked more than any man he'd known. Then it was Natalya, whom he liked so much he did not permit himself to feel any other thing for her. Next it was Sacha, with whom he felt a mysterious bond. Lastly it was Alice Miller, whose writings, once discovered, had empowered him to leapfrog hurdles in therapy, the very ones that had ruptured him. Miller gave his evil childhood a face, a name. It happened, she said. He was indebted to his four new friends, counting Miller, and yet he could not bring himself to share with them, or anyone, the psychic engine he'd built to ride his inner storms. He didn't wish to define himself irrevocably to them, to single out, to put at risk any aspect of what they'd come to share.

As the room changed shape the nature of their childhoods emerged. Natalya and Dom remembered the impulse to take cover from Cossacks, Nazis, parents. Paolo had observed children's penchant to hide, but wanting or needing to take cover eluded him.

"Didn't you ever build a snow fort?" Dom asked.

"No, just figures I poured water on to freeze," Paolo said.

But one evening, two weeks after this conversation, Paolo arrived lugging a huge orange sail bag, which Dom had given him. He worked through the night, falling asleep on the floor just before daylight. When Natalya woke him with a whiff of coffee he jumped up and feathered a rocker switch. A concave panel withdrew and then slid back behind heaven and a Kevlar tent fell like golden sheet rain. Natalya jumped back.

"I'm devising a spring-loaded hoop to belly it out when it falls," he said. "Sacha's hideaway, you see. Xanadu!"

Her face was a glade flashing darkly as marching clouds bar the sun. She brushed away hair that wasn't there with the back of her hand and stuck out her lower lip like a child catching tears. She wanted to turn, to hide the harm of this blast from a place beyond memory's reach, but her feet stuck.

Paolo turned to the window. His mind flooded in the eastern light with visions of his sister Anna's lovely face bursting into tears when she could not absorb some sight or gesture or word that moved her.

When he'd washed up he joined Natalya in the kitchen, picked up a spoon and began feeding Sacha banana mash, making faces.

"You're like my sister Anna."

"Tell me."

"She's an angel."

"She's dead, Paolo?"

"No, I meant she has this light around her, people long to touch her, you can see it. She's like a Madonna reputed to weep. People want to hold vigils near her."

"Where is she?"

"She lives with my parents. They were pretty old when she was born. She cares for them."

"She didn't marry?"

"Yes, she's married to Marco Troiano. He's a curator at the

45

Uffizi. He's quite a bit older than she is, he appreciates her. They're happy. Anna is a conservator, so she can work at home most of the time. It works out well."

"You like this man, Paolo?"

"Oh yes, he's an aristo, by birth and soul. Yes, I like Marco very much. He honors my parents and their daughter."

"I like to hear about your family. So decent, so good."

"God was kind. I try to repay Him by making things He would like to look at."

She tasted her tears again. "There's a theory God needs our sentience to savor his works."

Paolo fell silent. He sipped his coffee. "Then perhaps Dachau killed Him," he said finally.

She stared at him. "And if so?"

"I have to believe He survived. You did."

"Oh Paolo, I have to get to work. Anna and I can only bear so much."

What we don't know about each other is almost always what would benefit us most to know. And how rarely we choose what would benefit us.

A quixotic gene pool contrived to give Dom Maggiore one of those evocative faces—is it only his face?—as likely to summon blood to the eye as to the heart. The peaceableness of his life, such as it is, rests on his inspired perception as a young man that if he was to suffer such melodramatic responses in people he'd better be wondrously good at what he does and make damned sure it's practically essential to national security. Take the organizing meeting of a therapy group he joined several years ago. He was sitting chatting with a handful of would-be therapeuts amid a waste of empty chairs when a tall severe blonde walked in, surveyed the group, and then walked straight over to Dom and said, "You're sitting in my chair." Dom turned red, obligingly, and was about to rise when Lyman Heissinger, the therapist, started to examine the chair minutely while tamping Dom down into it. "It doesn't seem to have your name on it, Anne," Heissinger said, "would you care to tell us what this is all about?"

"I don't like his face."

"Well, that's a start."

That sort of thing happened to Dom. Or the opposite, as when strangers walked up to him with their life stories at hand or said things to him like: "You're very old. You will remember that we learned writing from the Mayans. I knew you in the Eighteenth Dynasty. You can remember if you try, it's important." He had no idea why he had such a face, but he knew he had it, and it seemed only practical to him to be indisputably expert at something so that having a problematic face need not spell job insecurity.

So well had he established this indisputability that today, sitting in an ostentatious Connecticut Avenue office six months after meeting Paolo and Natalya, he felt sorry for the hotshot patent lawyer who'd solicited him to study a formula that could under no circumstances be trusted to the mails. It wasn't scientifically interesting and was even less so after the gasbag with a carnation in his lapel subjected him to a ten-minute explication. What interested him, what hurt him, forced him just minutes ago into the men's room so as not to be seen weeping, was the receptionist looking up from her switchboard at a rondo of professional women's conversation before her, emotions of estrangement sweeping across her face: sadness, disaffection, the pain of being at once friendly and subservient, and a marvelous absence of envy. He would not swear this is what she felt but he would stake his life on it.

"I imagine all this bores you, Dr. Maggiore," said the lawyer.

He tore himself from the sunstruck window. "I'm sorry. It does, you see, because it's like wanting to patent the wheel."

Not, definitely not, what the man in the floral suspenders wanted to hear. "Uh, Dr. Maggiore, is it possible—no offense— that you operate in such a rarefied atmosphere that this formula strikes you as part of a commonly held body of knowledge but would not strike the rest of us that way?"

"That feels like a question in law to me, I don't work in that rarefied an atmosphere. It's kind of like astronomy. There are stars we've identified and others we haven't, and you don't lay claim to a star somebody else has identified."

"So?"

Dom watched the hostile question soil the lawyer's face. "So, no big deal. I discover things all the time that other people knew, and it doesn't make me a jerk—it's not necessarily a con." He sucked in his lips and gave the guy ten fingers up.

"Thank you, sir. Send me a bill, won't you?"

Nah. It'd be bitter enough for the client to see his balloon pricked without having to pay for the pop. And, besides, he'd allowed Dom a poignant empathy that sure as carcinogens changes everything.

That afternoon, hosing alkaline swallow droppings from *Nefertiti*'s lambent skin, Dom thought of Natalya's demurely bowed legs. Their exquisite concavity heated him like Courvoisier. What kind of man would defile the most gracious friendships of his life with baser metal? "Let it not be you, Maggiore," he said out loud, diverting his hose from a swallow's nest under the pier by *Nefertiti*'s bow. His mind filled with their faces, Natalya's and Paolo's. Then Sacha's. A metallurgist knows what coarsens tensile integrity. He smiled and resolved to clear the riprap breakwater under sail out onto the bay in a wind too high for amateurs, daring only what is decent and private.

You can tell a lot about men who like boats by their preferences: sailboats, putt-putts, muscle boats, cigarette racers. And the names—names count. A man who names his boat *Six Pack* or *Foreplay* or *Mutual Fun* or *Wet Dream* is a man you'd not want sober reflection to spare. A man who names his boat—a sailboat usually—*Dawn Treader, Papillon,* or *Ecclesiastes* belongs to a finer breed. Then there are the traditionalists who name their boats, sail and power, after women. Best you know a bit about the women before you consider such men.

Maintenance styles also speak. There are maintenance freaks who'd rather tinker, jape and shoot the breeze than sail on it—cocks-o'-the-dock who prefer catalogues to charts and fit their boats for voyages they will never make, men who let their brightwork go to weather, and others who cannot readily distinguish varnish from booze and consume both with abandon.

Booze talks too. It seems to go with gonzo horsepower and a lot more machismo than most skilled rag sailors deem safe.

Dom had the kind of boat you'd have to contemplate to study him. You wouldn't call her the *Nefertiti Sue,* after all. And besides, she was a gaff-rigged yawl, anomaly enough to keep twelve naval architects dancing on the head of a samson post for some while. Yawls are no longer popular, for all their grace, and a gaff-rigged yawl is an eccentricity of real proportion. Her black hull and burgundy dacron sails made sighting her an event. Chesapeake watermen were her true admirers. Racing sailors puzzled over her delicately, certain she'd stall in light air and stumble in blows, and the big wake-whompers put her down as a ragman's grotesquery. He kept *Nefertiti* in a workboat yard in Deale because he preferred the company of watermen to yacht club men—chaps with braided caps, chopped loin faces, and cooked doozies.

When he'd considered the properties of teak long enough he changed his brightwork—toe rails, handholds, hatch runners—to ash, and let it all ashen. This calculated neglect he tempered by keeping her fittings polished to a fare-thee-well, down to the brass rigols shading the eyes of her portholes. He preferred brass, which has to be polished, to stainless and neoprene, which don't. He was known among watermen as a fellow who never met an antique block and tackle he didn't want. Few of the watermen knew more knots than Dom and many had benefited from his willingness to make up fancy lines for them, braiding eyes and whipping bitter ends with marline. In some ways he was more waterman than yachtsman, and as the years passed it became rare for *Nefertiti* to go to the shed for repairs—so willing were the watermen to give Dom their skills. When his oil pump blew, the yard manager told him they'd have to drill through *Nefertiti'*s cockpit, rig a chain hoist and lift the 600-pound diesel a few feet just to get at the pump. Sorry, Dom, big bucks, forty-two dollars an hour, twenty hours at least. Wade Tillotson, an oysterman in his seventies, overheard this bad news of a Friday, said nothing, and next day came by with his dock cart loaded with tools and two-by-fours.

"Need some help, Wade?" Dom said.

"You get them Formica skirts off yer engine box, Cap'n, so's we kin jack 'er up and talk to that pump."

Dom knew better than to act surprised, surprised as he was. In four hours they'd torqued *Nefertiti's* engine off her mount, wrapped a chain wrench around her shaft so as not to lose it, disconnected the transmission, prized the engine up with the two-by-fours, slipped a jack underneath, pulled out the pump and figured to go to Annapolis for a new one. Dom held his forefinger and thumb up to the old man and they sat down in the salon with shot glasses in their fists and saluted each other. The old man laid some newspapers out on the table and began talking.

"Awright, girl, tell me what's ailin' ye," he told the pump.

Dom had busied himself tying engine hoses out of the way when he heard the old man say, "Damn to hell!" He came back to the salon.

"Ain't one damned thing wrong with this ol' lady. The sender ain't sendin' probably. Explains why the gauge done a header. Hell, this ain't more'n a twenty-dollar job, Cap'n."

It wasn't that an old waterman like Captain Tillotson didn't value his labor or savvy, he just couldn't see paying middlemen off the sweat of working men's brows. More than that, like his peers, he'd spent his life jury-rigging what otherwise none of them could afford. The fact that he effortlessly considered Dom a peer was compliment enough to damned-near make Dr. Maggiore weep, so great was his respect for the baymen.

"I'll go see if the yard's got a sender," said Dom.

Wade Tillotson found a way to reward himself in the perverse manner of his ilk: "Hell no, Cap'n! You jes' let 'em wonder what in the world you done, is what I do."

Dom clapped the old man's shoulder and they started a chuckle that lasted all the way down the dock as Dom set off to Annapolis for an oil pressure sender.

"The decent sort" is what Captain Abner James, one of the last skipjack oystermen and a devout Methodist, called Dom. "I reckon he's got no quarrel with man nor God." James was one of those people—couldn't say why—who liked the cut of Dom's jib when Dom first arrived in Deale and found a way to let him know by tipping his cap to him without saying a word.

Two years later Dom found the cadaverous oysterman mournfully ripping out the rotted strakes of his skipjack's cabin. He stopped to look and when Captain James nodded Dom said, "We could replace the whole cabin with aluminum and epoxy it, damn near maintenance-free." If James hadn't already taken Dom's measure he'd have said something like, "How much?" or "Who's we, Cap'n?" or "You a metalworker?" Instead, he said— they were his first words to Dom—"Cain't rightly complain, this here wood's oldern' my father." By this time Dom had clambered aboard the *Ellie Mae,* gotten his tape measure out and busied himself scribbling various fits.

"How long she gonna be here, Captain?"

"Cain't hardly work 'er this way."

"See you Monday."

By Monday Dom had fabricated a heavy-duty aluminum coach roof for *Ellie Mae,* lashed it onto the roof of his Ford wagon and hauled it down to Deale.

"Gotcher cabin on my wagon, Cap'n, need a hand."

He had to fabricate backplates and do a good bit of spot welding, swilling quarts of coffee (Abner James being a Tilghman Island Methodist teetotaler). And as the two men worked late into the night with work lights strung on the boom, Dom could feel Abner's excitement rise—as it came to him that a handful of grave nods to a stranger had given his well loved livelihood a new lease on life.

Dom made the taciturn islander clam linguine *a la marinara* and served up cannolis aboard *Nefertiti* that night, making himself in the doing a home on the bay. He also made cannoli addicts out of Abner James and Eleanor, his wife.

Nefertiti had hawse holes in her gunwales painted like golden eyes, a common Mediterranean charm that struck Paolo when he saw them as an uncommon gaucherie. When Dom showed up at Ducky's house one night with a chest full of big English standard-gauge electric trains he'd restored, Paolo determined to do something about *Nefertiti*'s whorish eyes. The next time the four of them sailed her, Paolo carefully measured her bow configuration, paying particular attention to her turn-buckled stainless steel bowsprit and bobstay, and in seventeen days he had carved and painted—and painted and epoxied—a wooden figurehead of Pharaoh Akhenaton's enigmatic consort that gilded her secure reputation as history's most beautiful woman.

His habit was to get the eyes right. With his gaze fixed on them, or just one of them, he could usually get the face. But here he followed the Hindu custom of opening the eye of the image when its features have been decided, taking its darsan, its spiritual truth.

When he came loping down the dock one afternoon with Nefertiti wrapped in an international orange tarpaulin under one arm and a tool box in the other, Dom was at the T-head. He saw that Paolo had brought something fond, and he felt like a boy who had a big-brother baseball hero who loved him.

That Queen Nefertiti was a magus whose powers linger down all time Paolo had no doubt: the task of making this innocent gift proved fiendish. On the night he started, he took a long walk around Fells Point and encountered in a print shop window, next to the tackiest adult shop he'd ever seen, the face of the only woman he'd ever been moved to think savagely beautiful. This silver-laden head of an Ouled Nail dancer from eastern Algeria ravaged his brain for days. He avoided the street in which he'd seen her, he fended off the thought of buying it for fear that the wild face, those shameless eyes, that changeling's mouth, would somehow darken the course of his life. So whenever he closed in on the tranquil secrets of the Egyptian queen, he heard the naked feet of the Ouled Nail, saw that gorgeous mouth, and feverishly conjured the dusky rest of her.

He'd always known that fitting Nefertiti to her namesake, sealing the seams and bolt holes and making her secure, would be dicey, but he was foolishly glad of this exorcism—to have her here where the sun is silver, not gold, where perhaps she would refrain from her smiling conjurations. His measurements proved superb. While the sealant was still drying, he shrouded the queen in her gaudy orange, this time at the prow.

"We shouldn't unveil her without Natalya."

He wasn't going to tell anyone how he had rescued her from any resemblance to the Ouled Nail.

Nodding, Dom thought how typical it was of their work together that he, like Abner James, would have regarded it as a false note to sing the queen's praise or to lavish thanks on her latest worshipper. Nor did Paolo expect or want thanks. They stood in the twilight on the dock touching the ashen toe rail as if it were her pulse.

"Incomparable womanliness!" Natalya pronounced when Paolo unveiled the figurehead. She didn't understand the silence that ensued until she scanned their faces. She would have given much to know which man had looked so stricken first. Then she knew they'd bent her pronouncement around to her, dismayed to find it imprisoned in their friendship.

Then each troubled their triptychal frieze. "Why *Mona Lisa*'s smile, which I've always thought fatuous, would intrigue men down through time more than Nefertiti's, I'm damned if I know," Paolo said. "Mona's a nebbish."

"It's the relationship with Da Vinci, it's voyeurism. If we knew who did Nefertiti's bust it'd be different," Dom said.

And Natalya: "You said it, Paolo, *men* down through the ages—I doubt you'll find many women more intrigued by *Mona Lisa* than by Nefertiti. Nefertiti's a queen, and a mysterious queen frightens men."

So their frieze crumbled, and they walked down the dock, Natalya in the middle, their recognitions keeping her hands at her sides.

Paolo's presence irradiated the tunneled shades of Ducky's house. She felt it in the walls and in her work with clients. She sensed it as a luminousness in objects. Because she worked at home three days a week, she stopped talking of the day when Sacha's room would be finished. Toward evening Sacha began to crane his head like an evening primrose, seeking Dom. In Dom's presence he cast away the mannerisms a child adopts to please or manipulate, and went home to himself—unstriving, contemplative, open. This calming marvel she knew to be crucial to what she might become as a person and a psychiatrist. And to what Sacha might become.

They understood in time they'd taken on the task of richly complicating Sacha's room in the interest of a way of life—a boon and stasis as Natalya thought it, a public secret. They embroidered the task in other ways, in noticeable but inviolate reverie. Dom for weeks had been caressing the savage edges of the wound where the door had been, closing his eyes as in a computer search, until on December twelfth, Dom's birthday and a Sunday, Paolo said, "Leave it for a while, it'll come to you. In the meantime, I want to introduce you both to somebody. C'mon, clean up."

"We have a date?" Natalya asked.

"Yup."

They soon were piling into Dom's wagon. Paolo piloted them to the National Gallery of Art in Washington. They forgot Dom would have to drive them home and himself back to Washington. Sacha struggled to get out of his sling and Paolo lifted him onto his shoulders so that together they looked like a seven-foot Etruscan ambassador to the Romans. The museum's perfect proportions—neo-classicism triumphant in its maturity, grave and yet intimate—cleansed their minds. Paolo led them westward where the robin-breasted sun lit a small early Renaissance chamber given over to a terracotta bust on a marble plinth.

"Lorenzo de Medici, Domenico Maggiore, who happens to be your doppelganger." Paolo bowed florentinely before Il Duca.

Lorenzo's brutally skewed nose called Natalya's fingers. Her teeth showed her amazement.

Dom saw the man he'd become, all but the scar high on the right cheek: the markedly pendant nose, the noble sardonicism more in the protruding lower lip than the eye, diagonal lightning bolting from his right eye into his brow. Andrea del

Verrocchio, the sculptor, had succeeded in painted clay in saying that Lorenzo's stare had been fixed and unnerving, banishing its surround as it did now.

"I knew I had such a face, but I didn't know you knew," Dom told Paolo. "Lucky for him he was a prince or that face would have caused him a lot of trouble. It's certainly caused me trouble."

Could you marry such a face, Natalya?

No guard came to tell her—or to tell her to stop tracing Lorenzo's thin lips with her finger.

Can you even take such a face to bed? Many a Florentine had.

The thought felt like pulling roots. Perhaps Dom's right: only if the face belongs to a prince.

Dom rolfed his face with both hands. When he removed them his face looked like one of Verrocchio's bronzes.

"Whose doppelganger?" said Natalya.

"The good of a being is to follow his own nature," Dom said.

"He said that?" Natalya asked.

"No," Dom answered. He kept his silence a while, then he said, "The stoics thought that. That's a stoic face if ever there was one, don't you think?"

They'd stood there a long time, at Dom's birthday party, when Paolo spoke. "Perhaps God himself—uh, herself—runs out of molds. I see it often. Certain types, over and over again. Too good not to repeat. But what's never repeated is the eyes— the eyes are God's true genius."

"Certain faces connect us with certain things," Natalya said. "You look around a crowded mall and you see a face that singes your body hairs. If you had to deal with that face, if you couldn't just buy an ice cream cone and walk away pretending—you'd kill it, or love it, or hound it, or break it, or all of that, and more. It has reminded you of what you fear or lack or need or hate, of the essential chaos behind all this chintzy order."

"Pretending?" Paolo asked.

But she'd lost track of what she'd said. "Oh, yeah, pretending—I was going to say pretending you'd never seen it, that face—but I mean pretending everything's still the same when it's not and won't ever be the same again."

"Just like that?"

"Absolutely!" Dom broke in. "A face like that changes your life forever. And you know that, you crafty Lombard, which is why you brought us here—but something in you is resisting."

Neither of them had ever heard Dom Maggiore speak with such penetration. Natalya lowered her face, wrinkled her brow and looked up at Paolo with a stitched smile.

"It's too frightening, too discouraging if you're an artist. Think of it, how many arresting faces do you see in a museum? Not many. *Mona Lisa*'s not arresting, she's aggravating. There's a lot of fear in art. We paint who's at hand, not just because they're at hand, but because artists have good enough eyes to know who's scary, really scary, in fact too scary to paint. The real limits in art are not where we think they are. Understand?" Paolo looked desperate. "We're talking about vortices. That's why you put your hands over your face. You look at some faces long enough to paint them and believe me, you're not there any more, you're long gone, end of your career, end of life as you know it—end of you, maybe. Who the hell's up to that? Artists are risk-takers, not fools."

The unnerving set of Lorenzo's jaw emboldened their contemplations. Paolo, prince of gestures, had only to be there—his work, like Lorenzo's, done. He thought he knew what Dom was thinking, but he didn't, nor did Natalya, and in that they were closer than they could have imagined. Paolo had not, as he thought, amazed Dom. Dom was not, as Natalya thought, lost in amazement.

Rather Dom was considering whether to hand them the single recognition it had cost him his life to come by. They deserved it, he had no doubt. Whether they could apprehend it, he had all the doubt in the world. And whether they apprehended it or not, it might one way or another banish their friendship. Why risk that? Risk is religion. Dom was religious. He'd hardly ever seen a risk—a real metaphysical or intellectual risk—that he didn't like, which was why he was always in trouble he couldn't even begin to describe. Just as he was now.

"The real problem"—yeah, he'd do it!—"is having the face of Christ, having people want to kill you with love, hate, contempt, need—you name it, anything."

"Christ—not a Jew named Jesus, but Christ," Paolo said, his questioning tone trailing off like the tail of a comma. He felt faint.

Dom stared at him with unabashed love: he got it, Paolo got it. He didn't know how well Paolo got it because he didn't know about Billy Salviati, Paolo's friend whipped feral. "Yeah, Christ, the terrifying face of God. I don't know why—how could I?—but it appears on some of our shoulders for a second, we never know when, and the consequences are always awful: we're betrayed, ostracized, obsessed over, raped, tormented, murdered...."

"Loved?"

"Never to our ease, Natalya."

A warning? Don't love me? Love me and be damned? Please love me? Love me because I can't love you? Is this something Christian that I've missed? We were talking about Jesus. Then he wasn't a Jew. Then he was God. She felt an abyss open at her toes. The abyss was there and she wanted to jump into it—and she would have, if she had not noticed Paolo unhook the gatefold of his improbable body and fold cross-legged on the marble floor, tired, as though beset by flies like a camel in a drought.

"Christ has a problematic face, not the face of some commissioner's sap, some mayor's toady," said Paolo.

They loved Dom. Problematically. Because they knew, they could see, that others, most others, might turn from him, hate him just for saying such a thing, and for being troubled, troubling. True, Christ might be a repellent Jew in a nave of Anglo-Saxon faces, or the face of Hitler's Reinhard Heydrich at a Hasid wedding—whatever is hateful, whatever roils the bowels, terrifies and dements.

"And each of us has just such a face to a certain number of people?" Natalya asked.

"I don't think it's everyone," Dom replied. "Very few of us. Most of us wear safe faces. Under warranty. They don't act up.

They don't get us in trouble. And it's not the face exactly, it's something brought to the face, some information. Well, that's both the right word and the wrong word."

Paolo found this twice-excruciating. Not merely because Dom wrestled with the angel or demon claimed by artists, not merely because art is more than the difference between the photograph and the painting or sketch—but mainly because Paolo had never dared to paint what he intuited about a subject. Inspired impressions, capturings, yes—but he recognized, under this great patron's broken nose, that he could not be the artist he wanted to be and dodge the metallurgist's face of Christ in whomever he found it. And obedient to the symmetry of his mind, he now believed he could be neither the artist nor the friend he wanted to be, unless he found a way to convey to Dom that he understood he'd been handed this royal recognition.

He must. Find this way. And maybe this put him in Dom's shoes because, maybe, he had to risk asking Matt Pieto if he had noticed anything unusual about his protégé Billy's face, anything other than murderous handsomeness. Of course he had—why else would Matt have befriended Billy? He saw now he'd always thought the reason was Matt's dark side, and he was ashamed. He was arrogant. That's what caught up to him here in the National Gallery, his arrogance.

Natalya, he saw, homed in on his predicament, or on as much of it as she could imagine. Her eyebrows bade him to enter a secret room. The Medici banker they had come to see was transmuting something here into gold. Not for nothing did the Medici harbor magi. They are still doing it.

"I can't imagine what it costs you to say these things," Paolo said.

"Fair exchange." Dom laid his lion eyes on him. Now they were occulting like an eagle's.

I could have been a Hasid saint and never loved so much, Natalya thought. Salt bit the corners of her mouth. She kissed Lorenzo's nose fondly and, seeing a reproachful guard, skipped over to him and also kissed his Nubian cheek, under the marbled glory of the place and the moment.

She turned to Dom. "This face of Christ—it's always disturbing?"

"No, it could be *Primavera*'s or somebody's aunt with a mustache."

"Nefertiti's?" Oh Jung, thou shouldst be here! She almost lost her focus on Dom, thinking of the old Swiss gentleman cobbling his stone tower together by the lake at Bollingen, pondering his archetypal dreams.

"I'll have to consider. I guess I just sort of assumed it started appearing sometime in the Christian era. Silly, isn't it?"

"Contextual, I'd say," Natalya said. Saying it recalled the gray Nazi spiders spinning their webs, lamppost to lamppost, in the Frankovsk twilight, twilight of the Jews. Her matter-of-factness became malaise, and malaise became panic, in the time it took Paolo, his leg joints snapping, to stand and say, "Feeling foreign, Natalya?"

She felt so grateful for his intuition she had to shake back a grand impulse to give him a mouth-on-mouth kiss, to let him taste her gratitude for comprehending how the very tears of Christ become from time to time the sea in which Jews drown. And she could not have shaken down this impulse had she not considered Dom, author of her malaise, whom she loved.

"Yes and no," she prevaricated, knowing it.

Marcus Aurelius, Stoic emperor and adopted son, thought Pilate a poor excuse for a Roman consul. So honorable was the emperor that he didn't see how evil Pilate had been—nor did Thomas Stearns Eliot almost two millennia later. It was Pilate who made inevitable the pogroms, the Protocols of the Elders of Zion, and the Holocaust. He mocked and doomed the Jews with a Solomonic decision. Dom and Paolo had few clues about Natalya's inclinations to such casuistries and literariness. But now she set this door ajar.

'If I didn't know you both, I'd say 'yes, foreign', but I think the face Dom speaks of appears in every culture, like the crucifixion—the face we can't cope with, from which we flee even when we love it. I have a client—he's wrapped pretty tight—so he put it pretty tightly. He was talking about a woman in his therapy group who'd asked him for a date. "It's no good, Natalya," he said, "the kind of screws she's got loose are the kind that'd crucify me."

She was primed to go on, but Dom took a short cut. "Let's not do it, let's not flee," he said.

"Let's not," said Paolo, putting a long pale arm around Dom's shoulder.

"Let's not," said Natalya, embracing them both in Lorenzo the Magnificent's glower.

At that moment she remembered heat lightning rumbling behind a ripe wheat field in the Ukraine. She'd never been west of Arkansas. They were standing in such a psychic field, far afield, lost. It had not gone as Paolo planned, had it? She wanted to put the moment in her pocket, to put it down as another strange thing shared by the three of them, but it was too jagged to pocket. She wanted a poeticism, but fished up 'in-process' instead.

"I call up the craziness in people. Then they want to hurt me," Dom said, just as Natalya had begun to suggest their departure with her body.

She exchanged a look with Paolo, not of puzzlement but of complicity. They saw in each other's faces that whatever Dom Maggiore called up in them, it was not an urge to hurt him. They saw hurt in each other's eyes. For Dom. They knew it was true, what he'd said. Some unassailable innocences invite assault. Natalya thought of John the Baptist and Salomé. Paolo wondered if he could paint the idea, or if anyone could.

Lyman Heissinger's plans for a masquerade reminded him of Dom Maggiore's secret—the secret that made Lyman feel trumped. The masquerade would be a salute to C.G. Jung. Heissinger's literary colleagues and their companions would wear oversized masks depicting Greek deities. Just the sort of party Joseph Campbell and his pretty Sarah Lawrence admirers might have liked. Well, maybe Campbell thought the Greeks were a bit mined out. Time would be allocated to brief utterance: Heissinger mused over which would be hieratic, which profane. He licked his chops over two delectable fillips: there'd be no unmasking, each remark would be like ink hanging in the air, and the party would be sex-blind, he free to be Artemis, confounding those who'd be so cocksure he'd come as Apollo.

Jung would probably have been intrigued by Dom. He might have tracked his feeling to its subconscious lair like an anthropologist tracking the yeti. He and Dom could have titillated each other with detail. But Heissinger was a debunker, and after seven years of pricking Maggiore's pomposity, stripping his grandiosity too, as he would have it, the psychologist regarded the jolting emergence of Dom's secret as a defeat. The cache upon which Dom's ego fed was exposed, as if Heissinger had found a vampire's harem at dusk.

Perhaps because the idea of the masquerade was grandiose too, Lyman brooded about Dom. For all his eclectic wiliness, Dom had eluded him. He'd smuggled his grandiosity intact past their seven-year struggle with Dom's depression. It happened unobtrusively. Dom took no responsibility. In response to Lyman's mere inquiring look he'd said, "D'you realize how much animal instinct there is in our everyday behavior? I mean, have you ever watched men sizing each other up?"

"You ever watched women size each other up?"

"Yeah. Same way, right?"

"We are animals, Dom. Animals. Whoever told you different done you wrong."

I'm gonna kick his brains out someday if he doesn't quit that hick shtick.

"I feel your anger, Dom."

"If you wanna talk yokel, why don't you go out and demolish cars for a living?"

"Let's talk about it, Dom."

"My dime or yours?"

"Hey, don't play gotcha with me, buddy. When you're pissed you move, Dom. When you spar you're stuck. Got it?"

They loved each other. How else could they spend seven years intimately, commerce notwithstanding? But they were at a crossroads, and Lyman deplored as much his taking the low road as he did Dom's taking no road at all. He'd not yet found the gumption to say the tough things, the necessary things, compassionately. He'd handed Dom a pick and shovel to exhume Tony and Sorella Maggiore, a gas can to douse them in cold rage, and a match to immolate them. Now he plain didn't care. He was tired of Dom Maggiore just when the aftershock of rage rattled their encounters, just as he detected the suicidal bemusement of a paying friend. How could Dom let him down so badly?

"You're gonna see a lot more anger, you keep trying to act like a guru in galluses."

"I live in Virginia, Dom, way down t'Occoquan. I'm just mimicking the easy way rednecks get across."

"What? Across what?"

"Okay, you don' wanna talk redneck, we'll talk animal instincts. Why's it got you so pissed? It ain't a discovery, after all."

"Lyman, will you cut it out, will you just cut it out so we can sit here and talk like evolved human beings instead of like a Nashville rockabilly baiting an uptight scientist?"

"What's this thing you want to cut out, Dom? Lissen to yourself talk, will ya?"

"D'you? I'm complaining about the way we deal with each other, like gorillas. I do get to complain, don't I?"

"Gorillas or guerrillas?"

"Take your pick."

"So d'you get to complain or don't ya?"

"Tell ya what, Lyman, you could have hung up your jock strap for a few minutes there and given me a civilized and concerned answer. Instead you just circled the enemy's butt, sniffing like a hyena."

Heissinger searched the moldings of his basement office for help. There wasn't much room of any kind. Dom stared at him, pupils shrinking, enlarging the golden irises. Then the eyes softened and moved off point. Heissinger felt like quarry reprieved. Accustomed to determining crucial tolerances, Dom didn't think his mettle would tolerate what was happening to him—what was going to happen to him in the next few minutes. Heissinger's mettle had already failed him. That was, after all, the nature of Dom's complaint.

"You know," he said finally, "I read about this guy—I don't hafta answer your question if I don't like it, right?—he commands a mission from another world and he forgets about the whole thing because getting born here mangled it right out of him—most of it, but not all of it, and that was his problem. See, they arrange to get born to certain people, wackos mostly. Well, wackos yes, but really their enemies, old enemies."

"Uh, is this relevant, Dom, or are you just blowing eighty bucks?"

"Bored, Lyman?"

"Fascinated. I didn't realize you read science fiction."

"I'm trying to get you to work, Lyman. You wanna work today?"

"It might be nice. Then again maybe not. Look, if you wanna abuse me in order to say something you're having trouble saying, then just for the record, it's okay."

"Scooter's a good name for you, Lyman. Run in and shoot and get out before anybody can assess the damage." Lyman earned the sobriquet from his high school basketball coach who thought him the feistiest li'l sonofabitch he'd ever seen. Didn't like him, though.

Lyman sat there remembering remorsefully why he'd come to dislike Maggiore. He had a face you resented having to think about. It's pretty close to unethical to work with clients you don't like, but what about ones you just don't like any more? He had loved Dom Maggiore. Now he loved him as the class dork loves the thin-nosed blonde with the circle pin, as a man who'd been tweaked, pinged, bluffed, raddled and in every wise trifled with and then rebuffed—just as the class cum laude loves the quarterback who patronizes her, just as the deli clerk loves the blonde mommy in the blue Volvo. He sat looking sardonic. He could not admit to pining.

"They're supposed to make a recommendation at some point about whether this planet is worth further study," said Dom.

"I can save them time. It's not."

"See, they'd already sent a bunch of missions here, some of which meddled and got pretty screwed up."

63

"Something in our air, I know. Makes 'em ignore the prime directive. Probably Adolph Hitler was one of them." He noticed Dom's fingers excavating his thigh. "He meant well, the little Schickelgruber, but ..." Aw hell, try to be funny, you hit the nail on the head. "Sorry, Dom, go on, please."

"So they're watching us, just like in all the UFO reports. But far from being ubiquitous, they're, well, you could say sick, because either some committee back home picked their parents or they did, and it turned out to be for all the wrong reasons. So here they are, picking up clues about who they really are, and trying to figure out if their mission has anything to do with their parents."

"Is it really possible one of the nation's top metallurgists, a guy with a wall full of honors and top-secret clearance, is hung up on Erich von Daniken?"

"Hey, I didn't ask you for your opinion—which, I might add, is usually like pulling eyeteeth with a tweezer. Besides, you're supposed to let me talk myself in and out of my own misery. When we started seven years ago you admonished me for my highfalutin language. I think you called it hieratic—sort of like the god Set intoning out of a pilaster. If I'd known your secret hankering was to talk redneck sheriff or racist basketball coach I wouldn't have given your admonition squat."

"It's Seth, Dom, I think it's Seth."

"No, damn it, I mean Set the 100-serpent-headed fratricidal Egyptian god, not the oracle from Elmira, New York."

Dom surveyed the room slowly, left to right, exasperated. This felt like talking to Sorella. You only imagine that, Dom, it's in your head, she'd say. She said it a lot—about anything that scraped against her uninformed mind. It's only in your head: perhaps all that enabled him to grow up bent but not twisted was his funny little kid's mind wondering, Where else would it be? Sorella's denial of her son's perceptions was probably what impelled him to science—where he could speculate, affirm, reject and quantify in white-coated peace and dignity. But he'd unerringly found a therapist to remind him of Sorella in the same way he'd picked his few lovers.

"Too bad Sorella didn't realize she could get paid for doing what you do."

"Ooooph!" Lyman had pulled up his rugby shirt to look at the spear when Dom got up and came over to him. He set his left foot against the overstuffed green vinyl arm and with a grimace pulled the spear out. He stood looking down at Lyman.

"If you haven't been wasting your time the last seven years, you're gonna feel better now. Otherwise you're not worth a damn, Lyman."

The most important thing he could have told Lyman was that we know a great deal more about each other than we let on. We think it's dangerous to read each other as well as we do. It's so scary, Dom believed, that at some point in childhood we consent not to read each other as well as we know we do. That is when we start growing up, becoming less than we could have become. Socialization walls us off from one another. These are the thoughts he'd been thinking lately. But Heissinger the debunker had already let on that he regarded such thoughts as magic thinking, subversive, regressive. It was unlikely he'd have ears to hear what Dom was saying.

Dom Maggiore was lost in a quarrel with his mission. He was the commander he'd spoken of. It was stupid to ask if this planet should be observed further. What should be asked is why its races consent to their terrible handicap, pretending to be less perceptive than they are. And if he knew this, wasn't his mission over? What frightened them? Why did the powers they were born with terrify them so much that they surrendered their powers to their parents like contraband, putting them at war with their parents? What induces parents to mutilate their children, generation after generation, like monks going out into Sinai and bashing their balls on rocks? These people choose not to face the consequences of knowing what they know so well. Why? Egoism? Don't they wish to surrender to each other? If so, only evil gods can appeal to them. No, Dom can't believe that. He sees the awful poignancy of faces whose words will not admit what so clearly shows. Panthers pacing behind barred eyes. Caged by their consent not to see, not to speak, not to touch. Some secret here. Something this place could yield. He has no trouble thinking these thoughts. Heissinger can go to hell. Dom has a lot of trouble thinking them, all the trouble he can bear, more than he can bear, when he can feel what others feel, listen to what they think. At those times, when he can do what he's always suspected everyone can do, which is pretty much most of the time, he knows the answer to his question. He can go home and report. The pain was unbearable. For that reason Christ was crucified. He'd asked us to be ourselves, to get real, and that is just too damned hard. We can't bear our gifts. Surely he comes from a world that can. A world whose entities—he can't call them people, can he?—commingle in the mind of the whole. And yet he can't tolerate even a scent of that commingling. It hurts too much. He'd consented to socialization, like everyone here, under torture. Lyman was perhaps right, it was something in the air of the planet. Which means we're all strangers here, from another place. A world where we know each other's minds seems to him at least the pediment of heaven. But when this heaven became practicable to him it seemed the pediment of hell: *Arbeit Macht Frei* on the gate of Auschwitz.

What did Heissinger know of magi and their work? And yet this quick, ferret-faced man had helped him wriggle out of the leaded leather bag in which he'd been tossed into the sea. That's how he looked back on clinical depression—an eternity in a bag under water, his eardrums broken, bleeding from his open parts. He'd cut his own way out of that bag, but Lyman Heissinger had shown him that all along he'd had the knife to do it. Great-hearted service, fee or no fee, and Dom wished now, brooding before the man, that he loved him for it.

"You wanna know what I'm thinking? I'm thinking ambiguity's a poor excuse for emotion."

"You're right, Dom. Whose ambiguity?"

He looked at Lyman, teeth locked, lips turned in. He'd settled him, knocked him off whatever smart-ass manic high he'd been on when the hour started. "So the way they come here is to get born, just like any other fruit on the family tree, and it's a rare aunt who suspects what's up."

Heissinger grinned. Dom looked sour.

"Well, this guy, the commander, starts to get flashes of memory. He starts remembering his mission. Then he starts remembering home. Not much, just a little, and it scares the hell out of him because the folks back home are shape-changers. It's like he's sitting on a jungle floor next to his wrecked plane. He's got a radio that receives when it feels like it and doesn't send at all. The birds screech whenever he hears something good. Now assume the poor bastard gets rescued. His next problem is he starts feeling what people feel, only in swatches, not all the time. Then he hears them think, again in swatches, and of course most of the time their actions don't jibe with what they think. He gets bored waiting for people to say what they think. In fact he finds speech about as primitive as his radio."

"Swatches or snatches?"

Kick that bastard again. "Stop listening to yourself think, Lyman. You're boring yourself. Listen to the story."

"I'm sorry," the therapist said meekly.

"The richer it gets, the crazier he feels. It's crazy. Sure, he knows that, but it feels right in a way nothing else ever felt right before. Okay, Lyman, maybe that's exactly how crazy feels. I can dig it. Now he knows—it's just a certainty that comes over him—there are other members of his landing party. Call it a landing party because he doesn't know how his own people talk. He suspects they don't. Fact is, he's got a feeling he's already met some of the party, like maybe one of them was the first girl he ever got the hots for. But they didn't recognize him, didn't even like him, and he was all hung out there liking them for reasons he couldn't tell. But he knows he's got to get them together somehow, or they're lost, and he's lost too, because one of them is the navigator. He doesn't know what's to navigate, but he knows that. He doesn't know how they're gonna leave, how they're gonna make their report: he's bollixed, which would be okay except that he knows it."

"Great ploy to use on girls."

"You can have it, Lyman, I'll give it to you and you can tell me about all the great lays it gets you."

"Sorry. Married."

Dom listened to his therapist concoct one non sequitur after another, bemused. He stood on a razor. On each side was Sorella, invested as if her life depended on it in denying the perceptions he'd entrusted to the only person to whom he could entrust them: critical perceptions upon which his mind balanced.

Lyman, trying to care more desperately than Dom could see, said, "You know why sci-fi has such currency, Dom? It caters to our infantile omniscience."

"I'm telling you a story. Don't you always say I have to do the work? I'm doing it right now."

Lyman leaned forward, elbows on knees, hands ready to catch the ball. "I'd like to know what's really going on here. What're we doing?"

"I'm telling you a story. It's like a story a friend suggested I read, Doris Lessing's *Briefing for a Descent into Hell,* but it's unlike it as well. When I read it my hair stood up. I mean, reading it, I thought this idea is in the zeitgeist, I share it with Lessing, she shares it with me. This is the way we apprehend the future. We don't go to it, we bring it to us."

Heissinger looked at his watch, not to tell time but to shake the sense his life was at stake. He was clearly panicked.

"What're we doing, you ask? Okay. I don't know what you're doing, Lyman. If I had your job I'd be bored to death. Metal's more interesting."

Heissinger recovered some of his professionalism. "Okay, listen to me, this is not the voice I've been hearing for seven years. This is somebody else I'm hearing here, and we have to talk about how long this guy's been lurking in the shadows."

"So, you can imagine our hero's predicament!"

"Tell me who's talking here now, Dom? You say this is a hero I'm hearing?"

He cupped his hand to his ear.

"We're all heroes."

"No, that's my line. You can't have it. We'll let me play therapist, okay? I'm crazy, yes, but I go to someone else to see about that. You, on the other hand, come to me. Now we have a third party here, so I have to decide whether to charge him the same rate, you see?"

"Hell, Lyman, take your selective hearing aid off, will you?" He knew the therapist was trying. Acknowledging a third voice between them flew in the face of orthodoxy. But he needed his anger for this venture. He'd known all along Heissinger would debunk it, but not that he'd regard it as abject defeat.

"Who's talking here, Dr. Maggiore?"

"Domenico Maggiore, or whatever the hell his name is. I forgot. Commander of the observation mission."

"Commander, I'm pleased to meet you." Lyman stood up and grabbed Dom's hand. "D'you think you could try to remember whether you have another name or some kind of descriptor? It might be helpful in locating the navigator, some mnemonic that might ring the navigator's bells. With a little luck she'll be a beautiful blonde."

"I see you're trying, Lyman. I'm grateful."

"Yes, I am. What I mean is, we definitely have to find out who you are, what's your stuff. We've got a whiff of civilization going here, so we don't want you stranded. Capiche, Comandante?"

He looked at Lyman warily. Lyman checked his watch again. "We've got to stop." He did his usual number, scrunching his brow as if he were sorry. To his dismay he was.

Maggiore got up and walked out.

Like a man who's left his luggage in a locker, Dom beat down the Canadian side of Constitution Avenue, keeping an eye on a smoking sun annealing Virginia horse country over the Potomac. He figured he'd skirt the Capitol and walk all the way to his apartment via the Mall, turning Washington into imperial Rome, its worker bees into tribunes and legionaries bearing frightful standards, wearing wolf pelts and marching barbaric slaves. Would it last as long as Rome? Artless Rome, so big on words and laws and viaducts, so short on beauty and worship, made him sob. He thought of a villa at twilight, its patrician, his veins opened, dying in a ripening arbor. He put the patrician in the time of Commodus and was glad for him that he had seen just rule, heroic sculpture and white buildings bathed in mulled sunsets on purple hillsides. No. This would not last as long as Rome. Would this be better? How could it be better? The question bound him to this unhappy place.

As he passed the National Gallery on his left, a perfect cetacean breaching a red sea, he asked his secret interlocutor for permission to speak. That was the protocol. Permission is not always given.

Will the mission end before we figure out how our parents are chosen? He didn't wait for an answer. It seems to me that's a riddle we have to solve, right? Like a navigational problem. Like perfecting the astrolabe. It's not conceivable—is it?—that intelligent beings would pick such people without a purpose. And another thing, I have the feeling I've already encountered some, maybe all, of the crew. What am I supposed to do about that? Walk up to them, introduce myself as their colleague and tell them the central purpose of their lives? I mean, were these problems discussed before we came to this booby-hatch or what? I mean, if you're just improvising, would it hurt to say so?

He was bemused and not expecting a reply when he got one. Do I get a chance to answer or do you just want me to contemplate your soliloquy, Commander? His interlocutor, called The Beloved in the Sufi fashion, was in the habit of answering Dom's questions, but not on Dom's timetable. More formal in speech, The Beloved nonetheless fell in easily with Dom's moods, and more often than not he was humorous in his dealings. Her dealings? Dom's mind filled with a toothy smile.

Contemplate my trouble, he answered. Give me some guidelines. Show me there's a reason to go on.

No answer, nor could he ever wrest one. Answers are bestowed.

How do people think? Is there this kind of dialogue? I hope not! Too slow. But it was exactly how Dom Maggiore worked out problems, problems that sometimes touched on national security.

There was his serious, polite voice, usually posing questions, and there was his profane, vernacular voice, sometimes wisecracking, sometimes just cracking—with sorrow and worse.

Nothing he'd achieved as a student, a scientist, or Heissinger's client convinced him that this demeanor of his mind was anything but adolescent and regressed. But he couldn't imagine living, working, any other way. At first he'd speculated this is how he'd discovered The Beloved, by inventing him. But the capabilities to which this discovery, invention if you will, had led him were too uncanny to be so pat. No, The Beloved was something else. Doors that couldn't be forced opened wide and handsome. Something like Hal in Kubrick's *Space Odyssey?* No, more like the solemn gods of Egypt speaking unbidden. Sufis say when the student is ready the teacher appears. That's how it was, and while he could never prove it, couldn't even talk about it to someone paid to help him get a grip, he knew The Beloved had connected synapse after synapse in his brain to settle metallurgical enigmas that had eluded him and everybody else. How could he not trust this whatever-it-is? Trust is fine, but he needed more than trust. He felt himself breaking up like a bad formula. Despair equals chaos.

His refinement of Code Viking preoccupied him, as it often did these days, by the time the Natural History Museum came up to port. *Nefertiti,* dear friend, apt coffin—he would sail her far out onto the southern ocean, charge her with timed C4, soak her in gasoline, and vanish like a Viking. He loved Code Viking as he might an exquisite vampire sleeping: some day, some day soon now, he would go down to her at dusk and kiss her lips.

A centurion would fall on his sword. Dom felt no disgrace. An aristocrat would fall asleep in his blood. Dom saw no reason others should clean up after him. Besides, he came from Sicily, where there's not much room between heaven and hell. The races of man fought out their bad marriages in the Sicilian, and Dom loved the idea.

He looked hard at the elephantine museum. Depression was history, booze was history, Scooter Heissinger was history.

Now his litany ran aground: Sacha, Natalya, Paolo, were they history too? The Beloved, spindrift of his mind, engine of his life—it no longer mattered—had made for him a bed he could not sleep in, a riddle he could not solve, a paradox he could not survive, a catastrophic dichotomy—only *Nefertiti* was sane, just, or possible. He thought of her serene face. Paolo would understand, wouldn't he? But Sacha? Could he get to that place under the Southern Cross without missing the child too much? Damn it, of course I can. Did I miss Tony or Sorella or Vince or Angelena that much? Did I? It hadn't occurred to him until now whether he'd missed them at all.

But the work Lyman and Dom had done deserved to be laid to rest—deserved its own rite. Years back, when Lyman asked Dom what he should call him, Dom said Domenico, even though Vince, not Angelena, had been the only person to call him that. Vince had always treated him as if he were a northern nobleman—as if Vince needed to. He thought he was beginning a new life by starting therapy and deserved a new name. So Domenico it was, until about six months when it abruptly became Dom, at first on his answering machine, to suit Lyman's excursions into redneck country. The therapist became avuncular, prompting Dom to rummage for warmth in their relationship, but he found to his dismay contempt.

Why contempt? He studied the question like an experiment that failed. What could its failure tell him? Dom never resented failure because it held out the possibility of richer successes. Nothing came, except unutterable sorrow. Had he begun picking Lyman's brain and nettled him? He thought of the Soviet psychiatrists, who to their disgrace had treated dissidents for their dissidence. Lyman suddenly became a symbol of the feelings Dom couldn't bear, other people's feelings. The Beloved affirmed in him the very things Lyman rooted out: the conviction he heard people think and felt their feelings. Omniscience, the grand disease of the unshrunk.

So he would go home, home in a black boat, crew or no crew. He could navigate well enough. He would founder *Nefertiti* as he'd cared for her, perfectly. He would tell her what he was doing and why. She would consent. In windless August she would drift bare-poled, but if there was a wind he'd lash her wheel. She would prefer it. With the golden sun-wheel on her black burgee flapping mast-high, with her captain-lover standing at the rail, it would end. Even if The Beloved would not belay or sanction it, it would end. At night.

Lyman had picked up his phone angrily, unaware his mouth was still flapping.

"Son, son, is everything all right?" Freddy Barlak said over the phone, mimicking Claude Rains in *The Wolf Man*. He and Lyman adored the scene where little Claude Rains knocks on his son's door, while inside a hirsute Lon Chaney Jr. writhes and slavers in his moonlit mirror as wolfbane blooms.

"I'm shaving, Father," Lyman answered, regaining his composure. "I just lost it there for a minute, Freddy."

"Got it back?"

"How can I help you, Freddy?" Freddy was an old high school buddy and now a colleague.

"I'd like to take an ego trip on your ticket, Scooter. I was wondering if I might come to your masquerade as Alexander the Great. I mean he did think himself a god, you know. Of course I'm not sure just how to look. I mean there's that fresco at Pompeii, where he's looking pretty bummed out ...."

Scooter giggled. And he kept on giggling.

"Scoot, you okay, ol' buddy?"

Big sloppy tears hung in Scooter's eyes. He was foolishly grateful for them, they felt reassuring. Pricks cry. Then he started to laugh. He laughed so hard he had to put the phone down. "I don't care if he comes as Alexander's mommy. Mummy?" He kept on laughing. Everything was so funny. Then he cried, and as he cried he felt like a good father holding his son's little hand. "This is a terrible place," he gasped. He knew he'd lost Domenico Maggiore, lost him when he started calling him Dom.

Some artists are verbs. The fewer adjectives, the better they paint. Paolo lived in progress between noun-lodes. He saw something complete and he painted it. Or he considered something until he saw it. Or he painted it until he saw it.

The first thing he did the night he returned to his loft from Dom's birthday party at the National Gallery was to rip down his big sketches of Dom and burn them in an oil barrel up on his roof. Then he took seven 50-by-60 inch canvases on their pricey expandable stretchers and arranged them in a rough parallelogram. This Stonehenge of surfaces he lit so remorselessly from the overhead maze of track lights that the canvases turned opalescent in their primers. Shirtless in coveralls, he took off his running shoes and stood in the stark space, sweating and running his fingers through his hair, reassuring his brain of....

He dashed off into the shadows, to a set of drawers, and snatched a box of charcoals. It seemed to him later—three hours later—that he'd drawn Dom seven times in seven places in a few minutes. Big shadowed faces pulsing out to the parameters of the canvas and, at second glance, retracting. The mad thought rose that the canvases wouldn't contain them. They'd escape into the darkness and live there. Giotto: madness. Christ: pain. Epiphany: no co-determinate. He observed the presence of more straight lines than he'd ever used for the human figure: ah, crucifixion. The light outside turned ultraviolet. He turned off the lights and waited like a priest for the arrival of Ra.

Eschatology: Dom had the demeanor of a man meticulously seeing to last things. His composed, measured boldness and his disregard for convention: had he had it all along and Paolo missed it, or did it involve them—Paolo, Natalya and Sacha?

He felt incalculably threatened, not from without, but within his psyche—hurtling down light years past galaxies and their worlds. He had not the sensation but the conviction of fabulous travel, sidereal, charted, purposeful. Nor could he imagine voyaging without Dom. Not now.

He doubted he would ever have seen his loft again, had Ra not come in his solar coracle, revealing the boarded mihrabs of South Broadway, waking the street Ay-rabs, sending Anubis and Set scurrying. Ra, no savior, no Prometheus, but rather an intruder, and an imposer of order. Order that Paolo no longer wanted or trusted. He believed he would never sleep again, nor ever want to, and he set out to prepare breakfast for Mad John Baptist of Ventura who lived in a junk lot off Portugal Way.

Mad John Baptist was more sane than anybody Paolo knew. In the night before he got out of the can in Ventura, California, he saw the pea-green wall of his cell turn pale, numinous jade, and he walked on through it into heaven and walked 2,000 miles, talking to joyous creatures in bejeweled villas. And in the morning when they released him, he thumbed a ride north, and when the driver turned to look him over at a light John saw a gorgeous ram with ruby eyes which spoke to him in tongues—changing his thieving mind and instructing him to baptize all living creatures not beholden to man.

How? Paolo had asked him. "I know that you will believe me, Paolo," John Baptist said, "when I tell you that I order them to baptize themselves. That is what the ram of heaven told me, and just so I would remember, he changed the color of my eyes." And when Paolo looked into John's eyes he saw blue echoes, reluctantly blue eyes, eyes that might have been brown, sea pools seared at the littoral.

"How'd you know I'd believe you, John?"

"Simple, man, simple. Your eyes, they ain't connected to your head."

"What're they connected to?"

"The beast, the star beast too big to see, man. I know you believe me, it's all here in the book."

Paolo thought of the celestial engine he'd painted in Matt Pieto's bedroom in Manhattan, of Giordano Bruno and his belief in calling down star demons, and how graciously he'd foregone the pleasure of inviting them to his auto-da-fé.

"The Apocrypha?" He looked to see what manner of red book John Baptist was waving, but when he looked John put it away.

"Think about it. Some day you'll be able to change shape, be anything you want, if you're polite, so help me. Me, I just baptize so they'll know, is all."

"Know what, John?"

"Know? I said know?"

"You said know."

"Know they're God, man, not prey. Know that men who kill dolphins and whales are predators, not gods. Roman soldiers with spears, masters of illusion. Got it?"

"Got it."

"All right, hold on to it, Paolo, Ol' John's gonna get you through this."

He'd been feeding Mad John Baptist of Ventura for seven months, one of those rituals that in time seems life-sustaining. John's thanks were always to curl two fingers over his ears to sign the ram, whereupon Paolo, always looking steadily into the man's shockingly fixed eyes, would make the sign of the cross in the air, like a priest at the dismissal, and leave.

Not the face of Christ, any more than real John's had been, but a crazed, disturbing assurance there to see. He would have to take Dom to see John. Good idea, Paolo. Or maybe not, for now he thought of his sister Anna with whom he could share everything, and knew he wouldn't share this, any of it, with anyone. It wasn't meant to be shared. Sharing it would be throwing it away, throwing it in the face of Christ.

He would bring John breakfast this morning, then go like weather to patrol the microclimate of his earth, Fells Point. He'd come here four years earlier to see Grace Hartigan, just to tell her he'd seen a painting by her that moved his soul. He'd left only to pack his things down near Saint Mark's Square in Manhattan and return. Rent was cheap, women called him hon, men said, Howya doin'? The place was clement, redolent of honest labor, and now—what? He knew something he didn't understand. For the first time, he was using strange, disobedient tools, tools from which he'd not yet wrested trust, and was happier than he'd ever been. And scared to death.

When he'd finished preparing John's breakfast and put it in a covered dish, he went into the bathroom, splashed cold water on his face, and did an uncharacteristic thing. He stared into the mirror.

"I'm Paolo Maio, don't you think? No? So who gives a damn? I'll tell you what, I wouldn't give a rat's ass to know.

Where's it written I have to know? I am that I am, let Paolo Maio be happy he's part of it. Okay? Ciao."

Silly for lack of sleep, he left to find John Baptist, left the seven faces of the metallurgist to metamorphose, disembarked the seven-engined centrifuge that had traversed heavens, changing his life. Paolo Maio, manic maker of celestial engines. *I am that I am may last/pit, tooth and blast*—his adolescent poetasting stirred like a paranoid's adrenalin. He smiled behind the croissant he'd stuffed in his mouth in order to budge the sticky downstairs door with both hands. Then, with his left foot holding back the spring-loaded door, he plucked John's breakfast off the third stair step and barged into the sun blank and expectant.

Whatever Paolo said, you could put it on and wear it, take it to the bank and deposit it, or woof it into the air like dandelion spores and forget it. Paolo had no secrets of which he was aware. Sealed knowledge, yes: entrusted to him and different. Omerta.

But Dom was different.

Just how different Dom was, came to Natalya on the night air as the lemon scent of magnolia grandiflora, in coded etching on its lambent petals, urgent as orgasm. She had been deadheading petunia trumpets in the dwarf Alberta spruce buckets out front when she heard the phone. Dom was home from his session with Lyman Heissinger, standing in the dark, oppressed by memento mori, unwilling to look. By the time she reached it, the red eye of the answering machine was blinking. She had to catch that call. She snatched the handset and dropped it.

"Natalya, Dom," she heard. She got it to her ear. "I find I can't make it tonight. Will you tell Paolo? Thanks."

Not for a second did his message seem innocuous. The radar of her mind, sweeping her psychic patrol, seized on a datum at approximately 175 degrees on the compass. It flashed urgently. Nothing westward, nearby. Southward: *Nefertiti*. If only he knew Natalya's mind often worked like an infrared combat intelligence center, or the main bridge of a spacecraft not yet built, Dom would have received it as manna. If he knew radar and sonar technologies were powerful metaphors in her work, that she'd assiduously studied such phenomena as echolocation and was a rapt connoisseur of such submarine movies as *The Enemy Below.*

Natalya opened the iron grille barring the sally port to Ducky's secret garden and entered, listening and watching. She touched the sepals of the huge magnolia with her middle finger, thinking of Sacha's long lashes stirring on his cheeks, thinking of the magical room, watching the radar sweep *Nefertiti* in her slip, hearing the sonar send. For what?

Dom Maggiore's secret. The metallurgist's secret. Something dangerous, rigged for silent running. She had the instincts of a sub commander, admired the undersea signatures of things—whales, propellers, hulks, intent, pain, despair—and could act decisively and, what's better, unpredictably. She glanced at her Swiss Army wristwatch: 20:17. June 24. Still light. *Nefertiti* flashed greenly in the vicinity of her navel, burning. Her pulse accelerated. The rules of engagement required nothing but that she should take note, but the secret protocol of good captains and all psychic black-water divers is that they follow rules only to the spur of their writ, where they then write new ones.

This squared friendship and exquisite stasis—Natalya, Sacha, Paolo, Dom—had a great, humming, blazing empty quarter in its center, and this moist night its writ ran out. No Freudian, she did not listen to analysands for seven years at $100 an hour. She was like her mother an interventionist, cobbler, mender, guide, compatriot. She went inside and called Helena Bedenbaugh. "It's Natalya, Helena, I know you can't leave Milo at night, but I have an emergency and I wondered if I brought Sacha to you, could you mind him tonight? I wouldn't ask except it's important, really. I'll be back before breakfast."

"Is something wrong, hon?" Helena Bedenbaugh knew Natalya Yasdarov as the most upright and responsible young woman she'd ever met. It never crossed her mind that Natalya might be wild to spend the night with a lover, no matter how it sounded.

"I don't know, Helena. I just have a strong feeling about a friend. I can't explain."

Helena had been Ducky's housekeeper and friend. Intelligent and kind as she knew Natalya to be, it was her superstitious side that bound them at a time when her husband's health was failing and he needed her. It had nothing to do with money. Natalya had often offered her a respectable pension. She believed her friend Ducky's child to be psychic and she wanted to remain within the sphere of that gift. She used to call Ducky Katya, but after a while she too called her Ducky and, although she never said it, she really thought of Natalya as Ducky.

"Come right over, sweetie."

Natalya grabbed her old Hopkins swim team jacket, which she hadn't worn for years, united Sacha with Babar, bundled his bottles and diapers, hoisted him into their shoulder sling, and set off for Helena Bedenbaugh's tiny formstone-clad row house on South Ann Street, not far from Paolo's loft.

Then she headed Georgette, her yellow Duster going on its third engine, down to Deale—where they appreciated such faithful machines.

She imagined Paolo entranced in his hospital-bright loft gliding from painting to painting. She knew it was hospital-bright from Dom's description, and she conjured a *pas seul* on roller skates between paintings and sculptures. How it would have amused her to know that in such states he mixed paints in his palm.

She thought of Dom, masked, alien in the center of welder's meteors. Perhaps he was there in his shop, and not in Deale.

There were many good reasons to think of Paolo. Thinking of Paolo was reassuring, but Natalya's one reason was that neither of them much disputed in themselves: what they were to do was good as done, like getting to Hairston's Boatyard now.

She arrived at Hairston's in ease of mind, padding down the long dock in moccasins, saluting a couple of weathered gaffers who looked up from the engine holds of their workboats, their chosen place of prayer—altars lit by caged extension bulbs.

The yellow dock lamps with their bug bulbs cast catenary shadows of dock lines on the plangent water. Hawse holes and pilings and cleats creaked and groaned as their lines burnished them. She saw *Nefertiti*'s in-port house flag—a green swallow-tail burgee with a golden ankh emblazoned on it, under her spreader—stirring in an east wind, signaling change as east winds do.

A gas lantern swung behind a smoked brass-lined deadlight, its mantle turned down. Wind chutes bent to *Nefertiti's* booms downloaded honeysuckle air into two hatches. As Natalya came closer she heard Puccini's *Madame Butterfly:* that incomparable aria of loss and betrayal. She sat down hard against a copperheaded piling, flailing in a wave of synchronicity, or was it parallelism? She felt twisted in a Hatteras surf. How could she have arrived at this moment? While Puccini was playing, perhaps, but at this moment of the aria? Attars of vespertine jessamine ghosted over Beckman's Cove from the opposite shore. Water burbled to the surface from below *Nefertiti's* waterline when the music stopped: the marine toilet being pumped. Then water trickled from a through-hull just over *Nefertiti's* boot stripe: a sink draining.

She heard the snaps of the main hatch's mosquito net being tugged. Dom rose spectrally, lifting himself with his hands on the hatch runners like a gymnast. He swung himself into the gangway. He was wearing a boatnecked undershirt and white cotton pants drawn with a string. He picked up something in the cockpit that looked like a harquebus, then he leaped with it a full four feet onto the dock. He liked to tie *Nefertiti* well out into her slip to keep high winds from slamming her onto pilings. Dom had the well articulated torso of a boxer. He'd been a fair three-rounder in college and the wardroom's token brawler in Navy smokers, his main advantage being a punishing jab.

Sitting in the shadows, spookily at peace, she thought of Lorenzo's nose, in profile, pointing to his chin. Dom walked to the pier with his instrument. He set it down on a sheaf of pilings. That he could do so indicated high tide, since the floating dock rose and fell with *Nefertiti*. His movement stirred a gaggle of mallards sitting on a crossbar of the dock beneath him and set them to quacking as they launched. Dom squatted and quacked expertly, as if he knew the difference between the quack of a mallard and a Muscovy, pumping his elbows like wings. A reproachful gull wheeled overhead and squawked at him, and this unlovely complaint Dom answered too. Natalya stifled a laugh. This was a side of Dom Maggiore she'd not imagined. She felt idiotically happy watching this austere man jettison gravitas to quack and screech and mime in the middle of the night. And she realized the gaffers she had encountered must be accustomed to it. That she was a voyeur, or at best a spy, didn't occur to her. She watched as Dom reached into his trouser pockets with both hands and began throwing pieces of bread to the mallards. The squadron honked and quarreled.

"C'mon, Oliver, give your mum a break. Didn't she save you from the turtles all spring, huh?" He aimed crumbs at Oliver's mum.

Your friend's conversant with ducks, Duckling. Yekaterina the mime would like Dr. Maggiore—evidently did like him. She felt Ducky's arm on her shoulders. Yes, he and Ducky would have had grand times waddling around, flapping their elbows and quacking. And feeding creatures too.

The converted Chrysler motor of a small workboat croaked up its carbon phlegm and straightened out into a steady putt-putt. Then, as it rounded the adjacent dock, the young waterman at the wheel called, "Hey, gotta a Bud for your buddy?" Dom held up his forefinger, then he jumped back onto *Nefertiti* and quickly reemerged with three beer cans in their plastic necklace. He tossed them. "Thanks, bubba, bring you back some blues."

Bubba? She'd grown up near enough south—Baltimore's mind is farther south than Washington's—to know bubba's a redneck honorific not thoughtlessly bestowed. She noted her friend hadn't said a word in this transaction. Maybe not unnatural for Vince Grifaci's ward. He picked up his sextant— that's what his harquebus turned out to be—and as he turned to shoot Polaris he sensed her presence. He craned his neck into the darkness and saw the moon reflecting from *Nefertiti*'s hull in Natalya's eyes.

"Natalya?"

She stood. Then she came up to him and pressed her palm to his heart in the gesture of a culture unknown to them, yet

81

familiar. Aliens recognizing each other, awakened from mishap and amnesiac disgrace. Outside her body she watched.

"I was sighting the pole star. It's usually all you need north of the equator. I'm pretty lousy at it. At least the dock's not rocking."

Her hand was still on his heart, or she wouldn't have replied as she did—couldn't have. "Why, Dom?"

Maybe he would have replied honestly if her hand weren't where it was. Or he could have said, Why what? or, Oh, to practice my celestial navigation. But he knew what she meant and by nature he was loath to prevaricate.

"I feel like a captain whose command is so expertly manned he never thought to do without a navigator."

Was he answering her question? A very great deal depended on not imposing sense on this exchange, on not fishing for the right thing to say. In the Dark Ages common sense availed and held science prisoner. Here sense must not avail.

She willed the winds of her mind to die down, she deprived them of their sun, and in that dumb calm she asked, *"Nefertiti?"*

"No, she's a surrogate. See, his command has vanished. It's there, but he can't see it any more because he can't imagine it. No, that's not right either. He can't recall it."

"The captain's an amnesiac." She'd not made it a question. Note that, Natalya.

He was not going to go fey. She brushed his brow like a mother talking to her child. It was his day for going on. He'd gone on and told Lyman Heissinger what he'd shielded him from for seven years and he'd go on now in the air of this approval.

"It's more like after a long time the poisons of the planet have disabled him. He can't function as it was planned he would, so he can't carry out his instructions."

"Does he remember them?"

"Not really. He guesses. They're benign, he knows that, somehow."

"Could it be that he's carrying them unaware? They're imprinted? He follows them like a sleepwalker?" He took her right hand in his left hand and turned to stare southeast into the harbor, where the moon had launched a million toy sloops among the wavelets and the reflected star-buoys.

"Maybe. But how does he get home? What has happened to his crew? Where's the ship? There are no communications."

He could be speaking of the predicament of her patients.

"Well, there are some communications, Dom—primitive, yes, but there are some."

Now, in the real and secret world of Dom Maggiore, they stood before the devil's anvil where he banged out tools inadequate to his enigmatic, immense mission. This eminent metallurgist could not find or forge the instruments he needed, and deemed himself a failure.

"Some cognac?"

She squeezed his hand. When he came back up from *Nefertiti*'s galley with little plastic snifters and a fat bottle they sat on the Cuprinol-green planks of the dock and dangled their feet over the water.

"Perhaps you have found some of your crew and the poisons disguise everybody. Sort of like ..."—she held her hands palms up and crabbed with her fingers for the words—"... the noblest features are distorted. Perhaps this place is defended from surveillance by an ambience that induces forgetfulness."

"Can that be good? How could that not be known, Natalya?"

"Well, a hunch ..."—that's what brought her here, isn't it?— "... will do for now. And as for good, whose good? What if the amnesiacs bring harm even if they don't mean to, Captain?"

"I know that I'm not a harmful man," he said bitterly. It sounded hard-won. He'd known harmful men.

"I know that I'm not a harmful woman, but we don't know how relative harm is." Her mind hurtled ahead. Good people harm certain people, she wanted to say. Bad people do good. Goodness can be harmful....

Stop, Natalya. Wrong turn. Her therapeutic compulsion to debunk betrayed. Therapy helps only if you can leave well enough alone. The better-read the therapist, the harder that is to do. Dispelling delusions deludes you, the therapist, into usurping God. Having done that, you start asking yourself, God? Who's God?

Can you prove they're delusions, Natalya? Have you got something better to fill the void? Something besides yourself. Don't mess around. She waited anxiously to see if she'd forfeited his confidence.

But Dom, like Paolo, spoke to the person behind the mask, behind the words, the person he'd liked and trusted in the first place, not the aberrant word or gesture. If these men liked you they persisted in it, as if you were the imaginary playmate of their childhood. You needn't feel threatened by your lapses. In this they were mafiosi.

"I have, I sense these abilities," he said, "that come and go, fade in and fade out. Something I'm supposed to do, been sent to do."

Where in alarm she should have defined the Jesus syndrome she exhaled in relief. Dom would leave alone what he'd entrusted to her, make no effort to get it back—to drag them back to more familiar ground. He would keep on trusting her. Dangerously.

"Then do everything in your power to hold those abilities, Dom. You must. That's the word from Zurich." God help her.

He smiled, clinked their snifters and said, "Okay, Frau Professor Doktor Yasdarov."

She had no intention of pocketing this exchange as a rosary. She would keep it on the table between them. She had not come all this way—by which she did not mean from Baltimore to Deale—to take his money and tell him to call for their next appointment. In for a dime, in for a dollar. Natalya Yasdarov signed aboard the invisible ship, signed the shipping articles in the captain's presence, and whether the ship was Sacha's room or something else again she would not let her costly, imperfect training deprive her of the adventure. She was not his therapist but his friend, with all the permission it implied to be as daft as Dom Maggiore. And just as brave.

"I'm glad you're here, Natalya."

"I picked you up on my submarine's radar."

"You'd surfaced to rendezvous?"

"Batteries. I'm a Victor Class diesel."

"Ah, the enemy."

"Well, I am a Russian, comrade."

"Is your sonar as good as your radar, Ivan?"

"Better."

"What's my signature? Can I see it?"

"You're clearly rigged for silent running, Dom—but in the deeps of my mind I can't ascribe you to any known power. You're definitely not out of Novaya Zemlya or Groton, that's clear."

"What's clear is you like submarines."

"Mmmm. Yeah. They're like people. Dangerous, lurking, foxy. I think a lot about *Thresher* and *Scorpion* lying down there in the dark. I don't know why."

"Am I dangerous, paranoid, foxy?"

"You're dangerous. Serious people always are. There aren't many serious people in the world, but there are a lot of schlemiels, and they're the ones we mostly take seriously because they don't scare us."

"So what was Hitler?"

"A schlemiel of course. What made him dangerous was that we took him seriously."

"A Jew who calls Hitler a schlemiel? A golem maybe."

"No. A golem is somebody's or something's creature. Hitler is us. That's what Jews know. I mean, what they really know. Which is why they're so truly sad."

He was looking at the sloops rounding the stars. And when he turned back to her, his amber eyes swung like compass cards in their pools, and he touched her hair.

"You're rigged for some other sea, Dom, some other task, and I think you're remembering it. You're something else again."

"So are you."

"What else, we'll have to see."

"And when we do?"

"Our ship will appear, we'll see it for what it is, we'll do our work, and you'll take us home."

Because they'd kept it light, because the moment was armed, she was startled to see tears trickle to that determined mouth. They had their work—his tears—to close a circuit so that psyche does not short. But because they sat shoulder to shoulder, she could not resist massaging his head with her fingers. "Home," he managed to say. He tried to sip his cognac, but her fingers and his tears were better, and he was trembling too hard. When finally he looked at her he said, "This is a terrible place, Natalya."

"Yes, so let's get on with it and be done." And then her words, administrative, struck her as end-world Triton missiles rising retaliatory from undersea trenches of despair. Let's be done with it, she said within herself, remembering harm first, then Frankovsk stinking with her father's breath.

To go below into *Nefertiti*'s teak-oil-and-diesel-fragrant lap would to another woman signal the possibility of intimacy—would be another woman's signal—but that kind of intimacy was hardly fit to wash the feet of what had just been consummated.

And so none of that crossed Natalya's mind as she went down and started puttering in the galley, putting on coffee, washing the dishes of Dom's last meal, and straightening up. She didn't notice the table top until she began stacking clean dishes before stowing them in their cubbies. Then she saw that Dom had cut and beveled a Plexiglas cover, raised about a half-inch by plastic dowels under which he'd taped a macro chart. She thought this a charmingly nautical thing to do, giving him two chart tables instead of one, until she noticed course lines crayoned blue on the overlay. They ran from the mouth of the Chesapeake out into the Atlantic, then south across the equator. He knew the bay well and hardly needed to lay in a course. She knew enough about charts from Dom to know this was contemplative plotting, an overview. An actual voyage would require a series of detailed charts, Admiralty charts renowned for handiness, big slick NOAA charts respected for currency.

The roots of her body hairs hurt. Her hair complained. Overhead she heard Dom securing booms against the east wind's warning, slacking off port lines, and taking in starboard lines to adjust for the swing in the wind. Somewhere in the South Atlantic, she didn't notice the coordinates, the blue lines stopped and a black *N* with a long descender like a spiked devil's tail had been drawn, and over that, like a diacritical mark, red flames had been crayoned. Not wavelengths or frequencies, but flames. She hugged herself. Then she splashed another cognac into her glass and was hugging herself again, glass in hand, when Dom chuted down the companionway.

"What is it, Natalya?"

"This! This addled piece of flat-earth thinking!" She shook as she pounded her finger into the South Atlantic. "You need a navigator? All right, you've got one!"

"There's this little book by Mary Blewitt...."

"Don't you blow it, Doctor. Don't handle me. I'll do it. You'll do it. Then we'll go home." Then she had an inspiration. "Wake me at 0500, Captain."

Question is, she thought as she undressed on hands and knees in the forward V-berth, not whether you're crazy, Natalya— you damned well know the answer to that—but whether he can stand the success of finding members of his lost crew. She laughed out loud.

"You okay, Natalya?" he called across the darkened salon from the aft cabin.

Now that's an interesting question. Actually she was having a great time. She's detected a suicide plot, proceeded to throw overboard the relevant psychiatric dicta, and was now cackling in a bent man's lair in the middle of the night. *Comme c'est drole, Danielle!*

"What do instruments do in the eye of a hurricane, Dom?"

"Completely unreliable—but you knew that, didn't you?"

"It's the answer to your previous question."

He didn't reply.

She was up about 0445 to find a heavy white Navy corpsman's blanket on her—and Mary Blewitt's *Celestial Navigation for Yachtsmen* tucked halfway under the pillow. The pump would wake him, so she left without showering, leaving a note on the table. "I consider it Navigation 101. See you tomorrow, Captain." She was halfway up the ladder to the cockpit when she backed down, crossed out Captain and made it Commander, his own word. Feeling as adventurous, as contrary, as disordering as Isabelle Eberhardt in the Sahel, she drove home humming

Greensleeves, lavishly rewarded. She had cracked a code, had no intention of selling it to the enemy, or giving it up out of patriotism. Where some other woman might have sauntered off with a piece of a man's soul as trophy, Natalya sensed her work set out before her. She was impressed but not awed. She'd not become a psychiatrist for what she knew but for what she had to learn. Sitting for a moment behind Georgette Duster's wheel outside Helena Bedenbaugh's she thought, Damned if this isn't better than sex. On the other hand, she reflected characteristically, maybe it is sex. Ready to smile, she shrugged instead when she remembered she'd always thought play of the mind the empress of play.

Dom found the eerie synchronicity of his last meeting with Lyman Heissinger and Natalya's night journey problematical enough to stay alive, like lacing yttrium barium copper oxide with silver oxide on a hunch that its conductivity would increase. More now to contemplate who would do it than whether to do it, he threw himself into their project. Or was it projects?

Into the load-bearing wall Paolo designed a 16-millimeter screen behind a sliding panel. A slide carousel in the opposite wall could be activated on remote. Natalya and Sacha over time could choose slides of the world's art treasures, he explained. The electronic details he left to Dom, for he'd found that whereas he was a deft electrician, Dom could turn electronics into chemistry. As they worked they taught each other, hands skilled as minds.

In time Natalya and Paolo noticed Dom stroking the rails and panels of the door meditatively. Paolo liked this quality in Dom, this habit of touching something upon which one reflects, cajoling the thing to surrender its counsel. Then one day Dom got it. "We can widen the entry using two retracting panels. They will appear as two black Lexan monoliths with the texture of a ruffled pond when dormant. But when their interior lights are switched on, Beatrix Potter's world will appear and move about musically."

In his enthusiasm he failed to get the idea over. Natalya and Paolo looked puzzled.

"Okay," he tried again, "the Lexan is a big sandwich, see. No, actually, it's a diorama. If you don't light it up it just looks like mysterious black panels. Tabula rasa. Sacha can imagine anything. It's his invitation."

Now they got it.

Paolo grinned broadly. Natalya pinched her nose and looked down thoughtfully. "Well, I can handle the architecture," Paolo said, "but you and Beatrix will have to work out that secret garden stuff." He immediately disliked what he'd said. He sipped a little coffee, then burst out, "I love it, Dom! What if one panel were devoted to Beatrix and the other to Ursula LeGuin's *Earthsea* people? Then as Sacha outgrows Mr. McGregor's garden he can turn to magi."

"I haven't read LeGuin, have you got her?" Dom asked.

"Yes. I think you'll like her," Paolo said.

"Alice probably likes her too," Natalya put in.

Paolo studied her face. And misread. She was considering the Beatrix and Ursula panels in the context of her night in Deale. She was combing Earthsea for parallels. Paolo saw dismay at the scope of their ambitions for Alice Miller's room—intimidation perhaps.

"It's a test, Natalya," Paolo said.

What is? she thought.

"If I were an extraterrestrial observer," he explained, "and I saw that a gang of earthlings without the help of government had embarked on such a project for a child, I'd report back to my own world that there's hope."

Mmm, well, that would depend on where you came from, she thought, or whether government is a galactic idea. Natalya brushed his stooped shoulder fondly as she mused. But when Paolo, down on one knee to grope his tools for a wire cutter, glanced at Dom—he saw a man who looked like he'd stuck a wet finger in a live socket. He motioned to Natalya to look at Dom. When she did, Dom was gazing at Paolo as if at his newborn child. Care left his face. He looked boyish. The word release came to her mind. Paolo had formulated the exquisitely correct metaphor out of the blue.

"Natalya?" Paolo queried, wondering at Dom.

She shook her head so hard her burnished brown hair flew. She chuckled and left. On her way to the kitchen she stopped at her bathroom. "Danielle," she said to her mirror, "this is an impossible situation, isn't it? We might grow old together with me a spinsterly sister or something. What do you think, Danielle?" She looked eagerly at Danielle's perfect Bourbon nose, her excellent Gallic face more wry even than beautiful—and slowly, very slowly, not to be misunderstood, Danielle winked.

The English standard train that he'd found in a Salisbury junk shop on the Eastern Shore needed reconstruction. Paolo had planned to use a much handier HO-gauge train, but the exuberant interior detail, the Edwardian mellowness of the Salisbury train, won him over. Everything now needed to be enlarged for the red, green and yellow train. They had to reduce the overall size of the room to prize more interior wall space from it. Happily the room had been a master bedroom, 35 by 20 feet, and did not complain. The Salisbury train wanted bigger stations and more countryside—and presented a new electrical problem. Where Paolo had planned to install plaster models of Kentish country, he now had to paint exaggeratedly three-dimensional panels on the order, he thought, of the Italian pittura metafisica school. Natalya and Dom had trouble and fun persuading him that the Salisbury train should travel only by day. That a psychiatrist and a scientific perfectionist insisting on banishing night distressed Paolo, and eventually he offered a Solomonic compromise. The train would travel out of night, by Sacha's left when he was in bed, to day by the window on his right. Dom was quick to argue that reversing Sol in his course might be malign. Paolo laughed, "If you think that's a problem, what are you going to do when the train reaches the window?"

"Oomph!" Natalya squatted on the floor in mock dejection.

"I've been thinking about that actually," Dom said. "I propose that we raise the sill, then we create a sky from the railbed up to the window, corner to corner."

"So the train doesn't stop. It continues across the front of the room, right?"

"Right."

"So what becomes of the window?"

"Well, see," Dom said, "the sky is the window. Actually all we're doing is deepening the wall to allow room for countryside behind the train and extending the window up to the ceiling. The sun rises on the left and sets on the right."

"The deeper Sacha gets into his room, the more it dawns on him. It's dark by the door and the train travels toward the light," said Natalya. She searched Dom's face for recognition of the metaphor—and found it.

The two men turned to study the window wall. Paolo at first had envisioned an oriel that would beautify the facade. That was no longer possible. Natalya came up behind them and, hands on their shoulders, said, "Cosmologists, can it be done?"

"It can be done," Paolo said.

"I'm thinking of ship's prisms in the sky—uh, the window—to refract sunlight into the room." Dom said. "If we don't like the effect we can remove or relocate them."

When Paolo and Natalya looked blank, he said, "You know the little green rectangles in *Nefertiti*'s deck—they're three of them, they're called quartzes—they collect the lumens and shunt 'em down below. They're lumen-multipliers. What they bring down below breaks up into the color spectrum. If Sacha likes them, he'll like Newton."

"Do the numens like the lumens?" she asked.

"Yeah, the numens dig the lumens!" Paolo pumped his fists and started dancing.

"Do the numens and the lumens dig the humans? Yeah!" Natalya started to dance too.

Soon they were dancing Bedouin-style, opening, then wringing a circle. They would have kept on except their laughter broke the rhythm.

Then they stood quiet, unseeing, basking in each other's light.

"I've been rethinking the heavens," Paolo said.

"Do you think even God does that?" Natalya asked.

"God's always messing around with stuff, haven't you noticed? Instead of installing a certain night, one that's date- and datum-specific, I could build a projector into the floor at the foot of Sacha's bed and then he could project whatever planisphere he wanted with a switch. It'd be a lot easier to do than our original idea."

Dom sat down in the southeast corner of the room with his fingers in his hair.

Natalya looked up at the ceiling, fingering her throat. "It's no small thing to give a child power to switch off the heavens, to summon them at his pleasure, and to reconfigure them at will."

Paolo's loony grin faded when he recognized that Dr. Natalya Yasdarov was not indulging whimsy. He looked to Dom for guidance, but Dom was engrossed by now in something else. "But our idea is to give the child limitless confidence, isn't it? We want him to be able to summon the powers of the stars, don't we?" He thought it best not to mention Bruno's fate in this endeavor. "The Medicis didn't abuse this power, did they?"

"I have to think about it, Paolo." She turned abruptly, uncharacteristically, to go. Paolo started to follow when Dom sprang up smoothly and pulled his left shoulder. When Paolo turned questioningly Dom shook his head, as if to say, Let her be. Something he fathomed, Paolo hadn't. Paolo sat on the third rung of his ladder studying the floor between his knees.

This juncture prompted the men to fit out for a voyage—away or from?—which would not always require *Nefertiti*. At first it meant sailing together. They'd sailed together before, but nothing was the same after that day in the National Gallery, and now they had to consider some parameters forming in Natalya's mind about the room, about its meaning.

They'd been somewhere secret, each of them alone, then together—and they needed to go somewhere uncertain. They had to reinvent their charts and tools. It was a mode of travel familiar to Dom, always journey-proud, salvaging from memory things he couldn't know. He beat to windward in his head.

Paolo waited.

Sailing the Tuesday after Natalya's sudden fear of Sacha's ruling heaven, Paolo gingerly skirted his friend's contagious quietude. The demeanor of Paolo's generosity did not invite overuse. Dom valued this delineable rarity. Paolo was not innocent, but he had an angel's inviolability. These men weighed materiality in their hands, found it malleable, unobjectionable. Mechanically adept men—Paolo at peace with it, Dom not. Not because he disdained materials or tools or skills, but because over his shoulder, out of the corner of his eye if he looked fast enough, there were, he knew, dimensions where such materials, such tools, such skills were primitive.

Paolo sensed an arrival en route, on the chill morning that a winch handle snapped in Dom's hand as he was trimming *Nefertiti*'s jib off Bloody Point. Dom examined the butt ends amusedly. "The process of turning iron into steel used to be quite a mystical concept. Not surprisingly, the Sufis are always talking about standing in the fire. They probably watched the caliph's smithies making Damascus steel, and they figured that's what you have to do to the human soul to make anything fine out of it. But even then it will have its valences and foibles. Metal is foibled—it's an ancient idea—and it drives people in my line of work insane."

Paolo was asthmatic with expectation. Natalya should be here. No, definitely not. If she were, it wouldn't be happening. What is happening? Dom is dropping a clue.

"The soul's like Excalibur. It won't come unstuck for everybody. Then again, it's not like Excalibur. Excalibur wears its specialness, the soul never does. I look at a soul and see ugliness, maybe even horror. You look and see beauty and hope. Same soul. Different eyes. Your eyes."

He cleated the mainsheet and went below. It was more than he'd ever said at one time about anything. He re-emerged with a spare winch handle.

Paolo sat in the cockpit by the main hatch, forehead touching his knees, hands clasped around them. Everything depended on Dom plotting some course, shedding some light, coming to the point, saying—damn it!—why they pulsed in a chrysalis, the three of them, waiting without knowledge or vision. He had not the slightest doubt Dom could do it. This was new information about Dom, revelatory. Finally, because he feared Dom would stop, he looked up to see lion eyes unblinking. He nodded.

It was a long time before Dom spoke again. "Three things have happened"—Paolo sighed in relief—"to our project, never mind for the moment what the project is—certainly not what we think it is, I'm sure—sort of like cooling steel in water, making wavy lines. The damascene effect. We see ourselves in wavy lines now, but before, our image was clear even if it was solid iron. It's like being a child in August. The wires thrum and sing and pretty soon you notice the world's melting—you know, getting all wavy with heat—and you worry that it's not going to chill out again. Not that chilling out is necessarily good. Children are always having these encounters with irreality."

This impressionist imagery pleased Paolo immensely. He smiled one of those jack-o'-lantern smiles verging on idiocy. An artist can appreciate a pointless conversation. An artist doesn't paint to make a point.

Hairston's had become Paolo's favorite sculpture garden. The logic of tools enthralled him. He'd unwittingly acquired a reputation in art circles for putting people on—pronouncing the channel lock and crescent wrench great works of art. If he'd just drawn tools, like Jim Dine, nobody would have pinned a tag on him. But from people whom society has assigned to work with their hands, declamations get them in trouble. At Hairston's, he decided the humble tang is minimalist purity, and Dom was often amused to see Paolo fondle cleats, dorades, gunwales and other nautica like an adolescent permitted by an indulgent guard to sneak a feel off a Rubens breast.

Admiring the dagger keel of a racing hull being power-washed up on sticks, Paolo asked Dom why he didn't race.

"Racing sailors look for the edge without. I find it within, where it's sharper and more dangerous."

"But what of the exhilaration?"

"Same thing. I never knew a racing sailor to say it, but it requires a certain recklessness, maybe not Lawrence of Arabia's kind, more like a gambler's. It's a bit weird to say, but I don't trust racing sailors."

"Is it an addiction?"

Dom didn't hear Paolo's question. Or it didn't interest him. "They want a yard to take care of their stripped-down machines—that's what they call them—but I love *Nefertiti* and I take care of her myself. I don't drive her. She permits me passage. We're polite to each other. There's a guy across the creek at Mudge's who has his boat hauled out after every race—hauled out, washed down, repainted, sometimes even patched and faired. Then they have to put her back in the water fast so the bottom paint won't oxidize. Costs a fortune, maybe two thousand dollars a pop. He's not a sailor. I don't know what he is. I don't care."

When they'd walked back to *Nefertiti,* Dom said, "Got somethin' for ya." He went to one of the many ditty bags in which he hauled propane bottles, small stuff, a sailor's paraphernalia. "It's one of the early mechanical fathometers," he said, pulling out a little mahogany box inset with a gauge. He set it down on four brass stilts. "I discovered it in the bilges of an old foundered lugger, over on the Eastern Shore at Isaacsen's, and restored it."

Paolo took it abruptly and swung away like a compass needle so as not to discomfit his friend with emotion. Dom patted his shoulder and began whipping the bitter end of a new dock line. When their eyes met again Paolo said, "It'll remind me of the depth of our friendship."

"Nowadays we use fish-finders and digital read-outs," Dom said. "Know what a fathom is?" He stretched out his arms. "Fingertip to fingertip. Don't ask me whose."

Paolo smiled at this evasion. "I'm going to tell Natalya what it means to me."

Dom, caught out glossing a profound gift with tech chat, repented.

"We should find one for her desk. She does after all fathom the deeps."

"Yeah, and after a particularly heavy session with a patient, she could tap the fathometer with her pencil and say, Hey, that was deep."

Paolo clapped Dom's shoulders. They laughed. Then it was the moment for an after-image in which to see themselves rivals—but they didn't.

Dom, *Nefertiti,* and Hairston's had become so dear that Paolo asked to be admitted to the mysteries of engine maintenance and moving gear. Soon they were overhauling *Nefertiti's* 37-horsepower diesel, talking earnestly of such arcana as suspending oil coolers with marline so they won't batter themselves to pieces when they vibrate off the engine block—something Dom had done once while hove to in a punishing nor'easter, after failing to round Point Lookout at the mouth of the Potomac.

The old Westerbeke didn't need an overhaul, but they took her apart anyway, cleaned and repainted her cast parts, replaced her hoses and double-clamped them, tightened her mounts, pumped out her oil, changed her filters, reamed her exchanger, reinsulated her riser, adjusted her belts, and for good measure checked all the electrics and rebuilt her bilge and fresh-water pumps.

They shared a passion for improvisation. Dom brought to it real-time intrepidity and elegance under pressure that enlightened Paolo—because his own improvisations were heated in a controlled environment. He yearned for this grace, detecting in its nature, in spite of the psychobabble of art historians, the quintessence of creativity.

Dom respected Paolo's grasp of systemology: how a thing works and when its working has been made rococo, hence fragile. Paolo saw immediately, for example, that roller-furling gear, which sets and stows a jib more or less automatically, can be flawed, and therefore unreliable. "Oh, for sure," Dom had said, "a sailor who takes it into heavy weather is asking for it. It's strictly for light-air charter trade. Truth is, the bay's so unpredictable, being shallow, I don't use it here either, though more and more do."

Such shared enthusiasms bound them, not as dockside gadgeteers, but as men who saw symbols and glyphs, clues to the access of meanings, tools for prying and sealing truths. Neither man was tolerant of superficial commerce. They'd have made little time for each other had they been. For example, Paolo one day fished a curious wrench with a swinging head from Dom's oiled and spotless tool box.

"What's this?"

"Oh, it's an Israeli all-purpose wrench. I thought it was a great idea when I saw it in Brookstone's, but I've never been able to use it for anything. It's diabolical. It always looks like just the right tool for the job, and then there's always a reason it won't work. It's my favorite tool."

The men, kneeling at prayer before the engine compartment, the work light illumining their faces, looked gravely at each other and burst out laughing, then kept on laughing at intervals as they pulled a zinc plug from the heat exchanger.

"Today we have some serious tests to run in your room," Dom was telling Sacha, "so it will take concentration. Y'know what concentration is?"

"Of course he knows. If we had his concentration we'd be geniuses," Paolo said.

"Yeah, we're kinda slow," Dom said. "Look how long it took us to figure out there's no Israeli all-purpose wrench for life's problems."

"Life's wrenching problems," Paolo said, unable to resist it.

Natalya was sitting high up the narrow back staircase listening, as she often did when she'd been upstairs. She enjoyed listening to Sacha engaged in their deliberations. He would look up at them and struggle to fashion responses with his hands. He would be one of life's enthusiasts.

The heavens as they were the night he was born, wired and lamped, were set in their vault—two fiberglass hemispheres fabricated at Hairston's, lifted up from the street by a hoist Dom had erected on the roof. A broad bay window—rather more like the view-screen of a great space ship—had also been winched up.

Nine compartments, each illumined by wraparound white neon, had been secreted in the floor.

Dom had begun to execute his wiring plan. Paolo had installed a city, a village and a lake along the route of the Salisbury train. Other scenes were in the works. But the wiring plan was hung up on Natalya's indecision about whether Sacha should command still other heavens. It would require a retracting screen, spread out horizontally from the ledge of heaven, to cover Sacha's birth sky—his destiny—so that alternate destinies might be projected. This in turn would govern the site and mechanics of his bed, which was to be raised to heaven's ledge with a bank of swivelling lights beneath it, as in Paolo's studio.

"The problem with all this," Natalya said, "is that no common tradesmen are going to be able to keep all this functioning."

Her words, voicing as they did her anxiety about the moment when the room should be completed, were deafening. The two men—working at separate tasks when she spoke—reacted viscerally. Dom pressed the heels of his palms to his ears and rotated them as if to unblock his ears from the effect of high altitude. Paolo wheeled his shoulders about as if trying to shake off a djinni.

Then, in a moment of inspiration or desperation, Dom spun around from his prayer niche between wall studs and spread his arms like a priestly celebrant. "This is our ship. How can we even think of abandoning it?"

If there'd been a clock it would have stopped. Their hearts did, Natalya's and Paolo's. More than Paolo, she knew the import of this moment. Mindlessly she'd precipitated it. It stood like a bubble filled with rainbows in the middle of the room, nothing a psychiatrist or metallurgist could do a thing about. But a catalyst, a magus, like Paolo?

She and Dom stared at each other, their secret there in the bubble.

Paolo was up on his ladder, his habitual place. He looked back and forth between the two below. Sacha in his crib in a corner actually had something like a bubble in his hands, a clear plastic ball that flashed colored lights when turned. Paolo's sidelong glance turned Natalya's mind to it. Her heart banged to see what she had imagined incarnate in Sacha's hands.

"We might as well hit the self-destruct button and blow it all up, as think about abandoning it to tradesmen," Dom continued.

"What button?" she asked Paolo, because she was so relieved and grateful he understood the moment.

"All space ships must have self-destruct programs," Dom interposed. "I've installed one but I'm not telling anyone where it is just yet."

"A captain has his secrets, Natalya," Paolo said.

Dom missed it, completely missed Paolo's reference to the ship, and to captaincy.

"Until we're white-haired," she said. "Then maybe Sacha may be told."

Tears broke like sweat on her face. She ran out, down the hall, down the back stairs to the kitchen where she pulled out a bottle—of course—of Dom Perignon. She brought it back up, but not without first stopping at her mirror to see who was there.

"There's no all-purpose wrench, Danielle. And we know it, the four of us." She pursed her lips and tilted her head to admire Danielle's nose.

Then she returned to the room.

"Champagne at eleven in the morning, Natalya!" Paolo cried.

She showed him the label.

"Of course. Uh, Dom, acolyte teetotalers though we are, we've got to pop this cork." He climbed down from his perch and took the bottle from her. "Glasses?"

"No, we're going to swig it like, like ..."

"Hit it, Natalya!" Paolo said.

"Victors! Like victors!"

Sacha stood in his crib, his eyes shining.

His last conversation with Lyman Heissinger started trap-drumming in Dom's brain. He charged them like a bull in slow motion, burying his head between Natalya's head and Paolo's chest, embracing them, bundling wheat. It was Nah, Loh, Dah in Sacha's words: Nah because the important people in his

99

mother's life called her Natalya, Loh because somehow the second syllable of Paolo's name described him better to Sacha, Dah for Dom because dah is so easy for infants or ... well, they didn't know.

The telephone rang. Only Natalya was positioned to glance at Sacha. Later she couldn't remember why its ring prompted her to look at Sacha. They let it ring. This moment, this embrace of their project, of their lives, was too precious to surrender to noise. But the ringing wouldn't stop. Dom let them go and she went downstairs to take it.

"Miz Yaz-da-rove?"

"Yes."

"M'am, this is the Noo-Awlinz po-leece department?"

When she returned to the room, Dom had Sacha perched on his right arm like a falcon. "Then tomorrow we sail. The weather's going to be perfect. Northwest winds ten to fifteen knots, visibility fifteen miles." Sacha listened attentively, always appreciative of not being baby-schmoozed. Natalya stood in the threshold, or where it had been before Paolo removed it.

"It's Irina. She OD'd in New Orleans. She's in a coma. They don't think she's going to make it. I have to go."

Dom pressed Sacha to him. Paolo picked up the paint-and-plaster-bumpy phone he'd strung from down the hall and asked information for Baltimore-Washington International Airport. He settled down cross-legged in a corner behind the ladder, his negotiations a background murmur. Dumbly she saw him pull a credit card from a banded pack from one of his numerous pockets, not recognizing that he was buying her tickets.

He rose, knees familiarly cracking. "I'll bring the truck up front in about twenty minutes. Your flight leaves at two, but we have to pick up the tickets."

She kissed Sacha between his eyes, her favorite spot.

Paolo gave Dom last-minute protocols concerning work in heaven, for Paolo remained by common consent the maestro.

"Call us when you see what's what," Dom instructed her.

As the plane leveled off its skyward boost, Natalya looked

down the aisle into the professional face of a flight attendant, and clutched her *Memories, Dreams, Reflections*—Jung's strange and moving autobiography. She had given her window seat to the sort of middle-aged doughboy who looked bereft without a cigar.

Without a moment's hesitation I have left my child with two strange men. Two very strange men. I didn't instruct them about diapers or bottles or bedtime or anything. I climbed in a truck and went to the airport without even thinking who'd paid for the ticket. Dom has to work—what're they going to do?

She ought to fret and vex herself, but she didn't.

Sacha's going to oversee the day's work. Dom's going to run out to Grimaldi's for food. They're going to sit in—my? our?—kitchen, chatting, feeding Sacha, making faces, dumping food on their heads to make him laugh if he's cranky. He's going to preside. Where are they going to stay? Paolo will sleep in the room at the foot of his latest project. He worships at the feet of what he's doing. Dom, who takes long walks, will take a long walk and sleep in the library where he can browse.

Tomorrow, the weather being perfect, they'll go sailing. They'll tuck the supervisor in his little seat, truss him up snugly in the cockpit and set sail. That's what they'll do. Dom will change the message on the machine in the library, he'll say leave a number, and when they've tied back up at Hairston's he'll download the machine, find out where I am, and call me.

But what'll we do? What'll we do about everything?

She closed her eyes and smiled. Irina is leaving. I'll do what I can do, but it has never been enough before and it won't be now. An irrelevant answer arrived. Why shouldn't Sacha rule the heavens? The Medicis would have done it, if only their artists had known how to let them. Irrelevant? I will tell Paolo to go ahead, to give Sacha domain.

She squeezed her eyes shut.

The Israeli all-purpose wrench doesn't work. It doesn't work, Danielle. Why was that so funny? Dom and Paolo too found it funny. It was no time to be happy. When is it time to be happy? The wrench doesn't work because it's not specialized. Happiness is specialized.

Remember the patient, Natalya, who couldn't help body-checking people in corridors, on streets? The poor man who giggled at funerals and laughed at misery, his or anybody's? Her middle finger was straight up over her nose when she felt her high-cholesterol neighbor watching her.

"I do that sometimes—laugh to myself," she said.

To which he responded, after her own fashion but with pachydermous travail, by touching her shoulder, which is to say, I recognize you're a nice person. I'm glad you have some laughter in your life. Thank you.

She sat back, her eyes shut, and that is when Danielle winked.

Sacha will be presiding, harnessed in *Nefertiti's* cockpit, yammering away. He'll sleep all the way home.

Whose home, Natalya?

Her mind drifted to Frankovsk. And for the first time her father wasn't there.

The Year Harry Retired

Every damned thing in the world went wrong the year Harry Noonan retired from the Baltimore police department. His wife Eileen celebrated their forty-eighth anniversary by dying of congestive heart failure. Then his six-year-old grandson Tommy was killed by a driver fleeing a drug bust. Tommy's parents packed his granddaughter Sarah and their grief off to La Jolla, leaving him with his.

The big guy, as his pals called him, had been a cop for thirty years, awash in human misery so long he could scarcely tell bale from bail. He never watched television. Couldn't match the incidents he wrote up. He missed the incidents. He was a fool, Eileen said, for thinking the police could do anything about them, but Harry always prodded the investigating officers.

Before they switched over to 911 and a central dispatch downtown, Harry was famous in the precincts for his write-ups. *The Baltimore Sun*'s reporters of an earlier time owed him a lot. Cops used to read his reports for kicks. But he finished up his days supervising the civilians who take calls.

"Even if ya don't, will ya sound like ya have a heart?" he'd tell them. "Somebody's life might depend on it."

Now all he had was grief and ghosts and the little row house on South Ann Street that he and Eileen had hammered, scrubbed and painted to a fare-thee-well. Not much to make a life, and in any event he didn't feel like it. So that first spring he bagged his uniforms, his medals and commendations, deposited them in a dumpster and himself on his stoop.

He talked to the usual suspects: skells, shills, bookies, deadbeats, wife-beaters, grifters, pimps, loonies, Section Eight renters, yuppies, rubber drunks, hookers, muggers, even human time bombs. He figured to do this until the day he'd find himself out there in his suspenders and T-shirt, and that would be time to get sick and die.

Then came Stosh and Natalie. Stosh was nine. His tow hair stood in tussocks and his tongue was tied.

Natalie, his sister, was seven and garrulous.

"Sarge, somebody broke Stosh's bike," she announced, hands on hips. Stosh stood three feet behind her, studying his shoes.

"Well, lemme see it," Harry said. "Looks like somebody drove over it, and was that a nice thing to do?"

"Steven did it," Natalie said.

"Who's Steven?"

"Mommy's boyfriend."

Harry got the picture. Then he got his toolbox.

"Well, Stosh, I fixed everything I could," he said after an hour, "but you'll have to leave it here so I can straighten the fork and find a wheel. Will ya do that, Stosh?"

Stosh walked backwards. "He will," said Natalie.

Harry spent a week fixing Stosh's bike. He bought a new wheel. He straightened the fork. He painted the bike. He installed a headlight and taillights and reflectors on the spokes. He put a basket on it and a passenger seat. And then he waited.

A month passed. Then one evening a spiny blonde with a shiner came by with Natalie in tow.

"Natalie, where's your brother? I have his bike."

"This is my mommy, Sarge. Her name is Mary."

It was eight p.m. early in June. The sidewalks were still hot, but Mary shivered. Her shiner was recent. She looked like a bruise. One of her front teeth was broken. A year ago she might have been pretty and, if born in Roland Park, even striking. He nodded. She stared.

He pointed to his eye. "What happened?"

Someone else might be blown off for asking, but an old desk sergeant has gravitas.

Her thin lips didn't move and he didn't wait.

"Natalie, lemme show you Stosh's bike. You like lemonade?"

Natalie came up, but Mary stayed put. "You too," he said to her. She shrugged and followed her daughter.

He poured them some lemonade and went down to the basement for Stosh's bike. "You take it to him, hon."

Then he turned to Mary. "Anybody ever does something like that to you again, I'm coming for him, hear? Harry Noonan doesn't fool around." A spavined smile appeared. She twitched it off and left.

She didn't realize that Harry Noonan doesn't fool around. But Natalie did. Soon she and Stosh were frequent visitors. In September they started bringing their homework and Harry started seeing that they did it. Before long they were eating early dinners with him.

The day of the suspenders and T-shirt was postponed. By now the big guy was fixing bikes, trikes, skateboards, wagons and sundry for a bunch of Natalie's pals. Natalie was something of a community organizer.

Then one Saturday morning Natalie and Stosh showed up, Stosh with his eye twitching, his cheek cut and a hockey player's way of meeting a body check. Harry followed them to see where they lived. On Monday he cased the place. About four-thirty, after the day shift at Bethlehem Steel let out, a gangly, sly man with a scruffy beard stopped and got out his keys.

"Yo, Steven!"

"I know you?"

"You don't wanna know me. Listen up. I'm only gonna tell ya once. Y'ever hit Mary or Stosh or Natalie again I'm gonna break every bone in your body and feed ya to the crabs. Got it?"

Steven looked like he was going to say something. Harry put his forefinger to Steven's mouth. "You ain't got nothing to say, hear? Say one word, I'll bust your chops."

Mary, who regarded words with fundamentalist suspicion and eschewed kindness like the pox, hadn't reminded him of his daughter Lou until she said, "So, hero, you gonna know me when Steven Dipshit shacks up down the street and I can't pay the rent?" Now she reminded him of Lou, the Lou of those

105

classically sardonic Irish smiles that says, *I doubt everything you're ever going to say.* He disliked it so much he could give up being Irish.

Harry's a lepidopterist of smiles. He knows which ones are common, which rare. For example, the cunning smile is as common as the moth and, like it, nocturnal. There is a rare monarchal smile—Maria's at the food market—that is so religious you can't find it in any of the paintings of the saints. It encourages you to believe, and not even his pension can encourage a cop to do that. He has limned the animus of every smile in the world. He knows how few stand up to scrutiny. And it strikes him now that he doesn't live in the neighborhood of smiles, but when one breaks out, it's a plague. So his demeanor towards his neighborhood, he sees, is exactly the same as his demeanor towards the miscreants who endlessly streamed to the station house. Does he have his daughter's smile? He goes to the mirror but can't think of anything to tease out a smile. The truth is Sergeant Harry Noonan never smiles as much as he looks quizzical, which prompts every kind of daft response.

Why doesn't his neighborhood smile? It blanches, of course, under the usual predations of the buzzard class. It grimaces in the shiny teeth of yuppification. It is confounded by the loss of real jobs, jobs that make things, and understands the service industry only in the context of a collection agency. He can't make Natalie and Stosh smile, not yet, but their mother Mary allowed a glimmer.

This gives Noonan in his noonday gloom an idea. These people have no one to report to. Nobody gives a damn what they think—even the bartender wants their money—so why even bother to say anything?

"So Mary, how's the dipshit?"

"Well, hero, he don't come home by way of Ann Street, is all I know."

Some days when she passed his stoop, which he noticed she did more often now, Harry thought she'd rather kick him in the teeth than open her mouth. Each time he saw her she looked older. "Ya gonna fix everything in the neighborhood, hero, or what?" she said one day.

"Just walk on by, Mary," he said mopily. Maybe this will be the day she'll throw that kick, he thought, as she wheeled over to him like a provoked biker.

"Stosh's little friend Anthony's half dead up to Church Hospital 'cause some kids beat him up back of Saint Agnes and took his bike. Ya gonna fix that, hero?"

"Ya gonna help me or ya gonna exercise yer face?"

Now he got it. Mary was angry and she had more spunk than he'd guessed. Yeah, she took too much from Steven, from whom she expected as little as she did from herself, but Harry had raised an expectation in her and that's why she gave him a hard time. She stood with her arms folded, her bandy legs spread.

He summoned her with his forefinger. She got in his face. "Ya know how to type?"

"I took a course."

He led her to the typewriter in his kitchen. "We're gonna do what they call an incident report. Then we're gonna give it a number. Number one."

"What, we're gonna write it on toilet paper, maybe?"

He held up his finger in warning, remembering how once when he did that a hooker bit it. "Jees," he'd said, "now I hafta get rabies shots."

"Siddown. Write everything ya know about Anthony. Everything. Age, address, school, parents, the bike, his buddies. Okay? Never mind how to spell things."

"Who sez I don't spell good?"

"Mary, I'm glad to see ya got a mouth. Ya had me worried for a while. Just write."

He watched her lean over the typewriter—she needed glasses—wondering how old she could be. He made them some coffee. She pecked away. She used three fingers, occasionally four. He went out back into his garden and pulled weeds. When he came in an hour later she was still typing. Finally she had two pages. He pulled out his glasses and read. He grunted his approval of details, like the style of Anthony's bike.

"You had lunch? Make yourself some."

Then he sat down and wrote:

> Anthony Pechevsky is six years old and is on the
> critical list at Church Hospital because some dirty
> little cowards in this neighborhood—yours and
> mine—beat him up and stole his bike last Wednesday
> in back of Saint Agnes at about 3:15 p.m. This flyer is
> printed on yellow paper for a reason. Don't be yellow.
> Don't let hoodlums ruin our neighborhood. If you
> think you know anything about what happened to
> Anthony, please call Harry Noonan at....

He put down his telephone number and told Mary, "Take this to the copy shop on Gough Street and get a hundred copies made on yellow paper. Then I'll give you some tacks and tape and you go put them up on telephone poles and street lamps around here. Here's some money."

He could hardly water his tomatoes the next week, he got so many tips. Two panned out. Nobody ever found Anthony's bike, but two boys wound up in juvie and Ernie's Auto Repair fixed up an old bike for Anthony and brought it to Harry.

People started calling Harry about break-ins, graffiti attacks, loiterers, arsons, car thefts, dangerous situations, noisy neighbors. Harry and Mary started writing up these complaints and giving them numbers. But then what? At first he made flyers, like the one about Anthony. Then he had another idea, a newsletter. He called it *The Crime Report*. He used the material in his reports. He asked for clues. Mary dropped it in mailboxes. She slipped it under doors and into mail slots. She deposited it in the forty-four dank bars in the neighborhood where a few old men in each bar sat listening to themselves age.

After two issues, *The Crime Report* was more popular than anything with advertising in it. Folks started calling Harry's house The Station. If somebody had a problem, people would say, check The Station, hon. Even the cops started making routine patrol stops to hear what Harry knew. It was evident he'd made an intelligence system out of little Anthony Pechevsky's misfortune.

This wasn't what he'd envisioned, but that's only because he hadn't seen that people need an icebreaker before they spill their troubles. Pretty soon they started coming by under the pretext of passing along a tip. They'd watch Mary type. She now borrowed Harry's reading glasses. Then she'd type. They'd talk while she typed. Sometimes, if Harry was out back and Mary wasn't there, people would just sit down and type. He told Mary not to number these reports. "In the old days we hid stuff under the blotter so the reporters wouldn't see them," he told her. "These reports are special, see, like witnesses, so we have to protect them."

Some days Harry could swear the neighborhood actually seemed happier. "It's 'cause you're daffier," he could hear Eileen say.

Steven left, but Mary didn't get around to telling the hero till she realized she didn't have enough money to make the rent.

"Forget the rent. You need to go to school, Mary," the hero said.

"Forget the rent, he says. Well, tell me, hero, am I gonna boff the landlord for the rent or what?"

"I don't like hearing ya talk like that, Mary. It's not the real you hiding behind that mouth. You and I know that, don't we?"

When he turned from the stove where he'd begun fixing a meal for them he saw tears magnifying her bleached eyes.

Her question hung like paint peeling till the phone rang. She took over the stove and Harry picked up.

"Pop, Gary and I worry about you. You know, you being all alone and stuff. We think you should move out here and live with us. La Jolla is beautiful."

"I can't do that, Lou."

"What's that noise, Pop? I hear kids, is that kids? Well, think about it, Pop."

"I have responsibilities here, Lou."

Harry hung the phone on the kitchen wall as soon as the conversation was over. His daughter Lou out in La La Land stared at the handset in consternation, repeating his last words. He stared into the yard where Natalie was gravely pouring Stosh imaginary tea in Lou's old tin tea set.

"Dinner's ready, Harry," their mother said.

Charm City

Peter Wattrous deGraaf crouched before one of Babe's seven full-length mirrors making Maori faces. He should have been practicing his speech to the Northern Virginia Bankers Association in Middleburg. He knew exactly what to say, what the chairman, Miles Richardson, Babe's father, wanted him to say, what befit the executive vice president and chief operating officer of First Bristol Corporation, merchant bankers, to say. But he was having a hard time shaving the face he'd just seen. It was not his face.

It was time to hurry. He nicked the Wattrous cheekbone. His mother's. He nicked the deGraaf chin. Then he applied a styptic line of Hudson River Dutch to the nicks. He made another Maori face. What he wanted to do was mount that rostrum and make faces.

Babe—nobody called her Barbara after Vassar ran out of athletic laurels to give her—was at the chairman's farm riding Bozo. But she'd be at tonight's affair for the speaker of the House, cheering on her thoughtful, excellent husband. Stacy would be there too, their beautiful daughter who would stare at him as if he'd been let into the club by mistake just as she had since she could focus her eyes. Perhaps Stacy would like this other face. Don't get your hopes up, deGraaf, the kid's thirteen years old and she hasn't found anything to approve yet. He never told Babe, who wanted a boy, that he just couldn't face another extraterrestrial stare.

The face he'd been shaving was drawn, darkened by the events of the day. A few hours ago he'd returned from Baltimore, where he'd taken his binoculars for repair.

"Mister, mister, how many times I haf to tell you Zeiss did not make these binoculars, Zeiss made these field glasses. If you don't understand, I don't fix dem, ja?"

He'd been bringing Meinrod Schoenemann his grandfather's antique *fernglaser* for years, like all Bay sailors who know their stuff. He had a pair of armored Nikon marine glasses that were the proper field and magnification—seven by fifty—for sailing, but his grandfather had taken the *fernglaser* as spoils of war and he was foolishly attached to them.

Not until today had Meinrod told him his story, how he'd been a young farmer in Silesia when the Nazis rose to power.

"Ute, I said, these men are no good, so ve go. Vere ve go, Meinrod? she said. I don't know, we just gotta go. So here ve are. I don't vant to farm no more because you haf to haf too much money to start, so I study optics. But I don't like eyeglasses, tings like dat. I tinker, dat's vut I do, I tinker. So I start Patapsco Optics."

"You and Ute just walked out?"

"Ja. She vus a good girl, like now. She know bad men when she see them."

"And what did you do when the war came, Meinrod?"

"Vell, I am strong, so I fight. Vus goot for the Army when they see I speak Cherman because ve take lotsa prisoners all over the place and most of dem jus scared boys like I vus."

"When will you have them, Meinrod?"

"I haf dem when I haf dem. You think it's like doze dumb cameras you throw away? I got to find pieces, I got to look. I haf dem when I haf dem."

He had always liked the old man. Now he was moved to embrace him. Meinrod was an enrollee in Peter's secret coterie of genuine articles: gum-snapping waitresses, ornery mechanics, acrobatic riggers, pesky sail makers, perverse oyster men, people he loved and cared about. He had inherited his father's sixty-four-foot Swan with its hoary old Rhodes diesel. He and his father had sailed *Roseate Tern* all over northern Europe. Her low white hull and dusty rose sails distinguished her. Now he kept her at Hartge's in Galesville and was one of the few bay sailors who dared to single-hand such a big boat. Like his father, he eschewed gadgetry, knowing that only the toughest and simplest mechanical gear survives the bay's notorious rogue squalls.

Blocks of sunlight and rain clouds gouached the city as he left Patapsco Optics, disordering his senses. He felt giddy, slapstick. Slapstick, scat and gibberish were Peter's secret vices. Given a phrase he liked, he'd spoonerize it. Nobody ever caught him indulging these vices, but his sister Lise, who had all the hauteur of their mother and none of his bonhomie, suspected them. She told him once, "I love you extravagantly, Peter, because you're so senselessly cheerful."

So, outside Meinrod Schoenemann's shop he put his circled thumbs and forefingers to his eyes, tooled the focusing ring with his middle finger and scanned. What he scanned at such moments he couldn't say. He had to see a thing to understand it, which is why banking, being conceptual, bored him. His thumb-and-forefinger binoculars invaded the realities where Peter performed his brain's virtual surgeries, traversed stars and cut the Gordian knot. When he put them down he knew what to do.

He left his Beamer where he shouldn't have and started walking down Twenty-Fourth Street towards Saint Paul's. In two more blocks he came upon Saint Michael and All Angels, a Romanesque Episcopal church standing sheepishly triumphal in the midst of horrific squalor. Some homeless men were vetting visitors with a vengeance. Peter stood across the street in a light rain, adjusting his virtual binoculars. A cop on a bicycle rode up, dismounted and wheeled his bike into a tiny substation in the groin of the church. A bell rang and in less than a minute a long bedraggled line formed outside. He watched the church devour it. Then he walked two more blocks down to North Avenue. Once-grand houses were nailed shut, leaning on each other, starved for care. Grungy curtains blew out of broken windows. Spray-paint graffiti groped out in grotesque arabesques to choke a demoralized citizenry. A man tumbled out from behind a boarded-up plywood door, his left foot flopping hapless. By a series of pratfalls he negotiated the steps and plopped onto the bottom step with a bone-breaking jar. Syphilis, Peter thought. Probably ranks with a bad cold in these parts. The door had been stenciled:

PRIVATE PROPERTY
NO LOITERING
NO TRESPASSING
IF ANIMAL TRAPPED
INSIDE CALL 396-6286

He began talking in his head, as he often did. Now I know who to call about the animal trapped inside. I have visited Meinrod's Magical Optics Shoppe and now I see things differently. Now you see things, Peter, he corrected himself. But I always did, didn't I? We have an underclass, yes. What society doesn't? Most of the wealth is in the hands of one percent of the population— yes—but they invest it to our benefit, don't they? You believe that, Peter? Did Ronald Reagan believe it? Well, let's say he acted as if he did. Peter had never met a banker who believed it, nor had he ever met one who was unhappy that the Speaker of the House did.

Lost in his head, he smacked right into an offer of a five-dollar blow job. "Ya got ten, hon, ya can do anything," she said helpfully.

Hey, stupid, you know where you are? A honky in a four-thousand-dollar suit on North Avenue? Yeah, I know where I am—John Wilkes Booth is buried across the street, eternally baffled by history's ingratitude.

He gave her a ten. She took his arm and tugged him towards an alley. He picked her arm off. "Keep it, it's okay." What a smile! Not for his generosity but for his stupidity.

He crossed the avenue to Greenmount Cemetery. Over the cairn-like wall he could make out the first row of stones. Most of the inhabitants had lived in these hog-backed and cracked mansions. They too believed in the trickling down of largesse— or said they did. He turned down Patterson Park Avenue and encountered a teenager with a shiner. She couldn't have been more than sixteen, pushing a kid, making another. Sallow. From her two front teeth back she was missing at least two more. Her blue eyes looked as if they'd been rinsed in xylol. Jesus! Was she going to proposition him? Well, that's what you get for staring.

"You got any money, hon?"

If he'd thought of something to say on North Avenue he was tongue-tied by now. He looked down at the child. A crone looked back from behind a baby mask—older than the mother, sadder but less frightened. What does crack addiction look like?

"Whuddya like, Mister? I'm clean."

Peter reached for his wallet, but he found himself arguing with trickle-down economics by trying to crawl into his inside pocket. He spun away from the girl and started brushing raindrops from his jacket to find they were tears. This girl tugged his arm. "You all right, hon?" He turned and looked at her with something like love. He knew in that instant he'd never looked at Babe like that.

"What's your name?"

"Dawn."

"Dawn," he said. A cobalt sob burned his lungs. "Here, Dawn, I won the lottery, I feel a little crazy, take care of yourself." He gave her a hundred and eighty-three dollars, all he had in his wallet, and walked away.

He found his Beamer, the one with Babe's Ollie by Golly bumper sticker, the one he'd merrily driven to the polls to vote for Chuck Robb. By pure luck it was still intact. He drove around Charm City, its broken stoops, charred row houses, topless dance holes, decrepit schools, toppled cemeteries, swastikas, scuttling beer cans and muscatel bottles, needles lurking in the gutters, vineyards of junk and hubcap blossoms, leprous clunkers, toreador pedestrians, kamikaze bike couriers.

He stopped at the corner of a blasted intersection where not even the streetlight worked. One incongruously hale but boarded-up row house stood out from the ruins. An almost new sign said, "Sidney Cohen, Dentist." He parked and stared like a Zen archer. The arrow of his mind hit an odd thought—to survive here is a kind of exile. Was Sidney Cohen a bright young man who'd set up here to serve the poor but gotten discouraged, even robbed or beaten? Was he an old man, perhaps a Holocaust survivor who'd stayed as the neighborhood sickened with liens and defaults and neglect? Where was Sidney Cohen?

Peter had no idea why the grand salon in the Middleburg Inn is the Cormorant Room. It's horse country, after all. A sailor and bird watcher, he should appreciate it. Instead he chewed the awryness of things, expatriate, like T.E. Lawrence towing a djellabahed wog into the officers' club in Cairo. When he got inside the place he felt hoodooed by covens of Stacies.

Well, one thing, pal, you don't have to ad-lib. It's a canned speech.

Was that what he was afraid of?

"Ah, the man of the hour!" the chairman cried on seeing him. "I want you to come say hello to the Speaker. He's an admirer of yours, Peter."

"I must have done something awful."

The chairman feigned a chuckle. "I always knew I could leave it to Babe to find a man with a sense of humor. Downsizing, Peter, he admires the way you downsized a bloated First Bristol."

"I see. Shall I mention Barings Bank, Miles?" He never called the chairman Miles.

"Barings? Why would you do a thing like that? Oh, you're joking again. What am I going to do with you, lad?" Miles never called him lad.

"Well, it's entirely possible we have a Nick Leeson in our midst, Miles."

"Then find him and fire the son of a bitch!"

Peter was impressed, he had to admit, that his proudly unread father-in-law was even remotely aware that a baby-faced grammar school dropout had ruined the hoity-toitiest bank in England by his incredibly unsupervised churning and burning. The chairman's ignorance of banking was encyclopedic and, besides, a crackling thatch of hair was pitching towards them.

"Mr. Speaker, this is my son-in-law, Pete deGraaf. Whatever you want to know about banking, just ask Pete. We're on your side, sir."

"It's a pleasure, Mr. deGraaf. I want to hear about how you downsized First Bristol. We want to learn all we can about how the private sector operates without the problems we encounter in government."

"It doesn't."

"Mr. Speaker, I must warn you, my son-in-law is a card. He'll put you on till it hurts."

"It doesn't hurt, Miles, no indeed. I'm all ears. For example, Mr. deGraaf, the Barings thing, could it happen here?"

"In one form or another it already has, Mr. Speaker. We've had a premier bank in insolvency for several years. I should think they would have let you in on the secret, sir."

The chairman was unable to shut his bile duct. Peter forced his eyes down from the Speaker's hair to the eyes. They were as secret as the insolvency he'd mentioned. The Speaker did the only thing a gentleman could do. "I'll be very interested in what you have to say tonight, Mr. deGraaf, and I'd like to continue this conversation at your convenience." Peter nodded. The Speaker recirculated.

"What in God's name were you thinking, Peter?" The chairman peered into his face as if sun-blinded. This maneuver earned the chairman his first look at the severity of the deGraafs and the haughtiness of the Wattrouses. The chairman knew it was time to repair to the bar, where nothing is repaired. Peter's look rode him all the way.

The stranger masquerading as Peter deGraaf studied the Speaker of the House from the rostrum. He saw love and fear and was ambushed by compassion. He heard T. Wallace Hyde, the president of the association, introduce him as "one of the men who will lead our banking industry boldly into a twenty-first century unfettered by government snoops" when his pale eyes fell on the outlaw legs and depravedly erotic face of Kelly Meyerson. Babe's pal and agent provocateur, Kelly drank too much, ran around on her husband Wilfred and preferred women to members of what she called the dipshit species. Peter thought of Wilfred, the chairman's hand-picked auditor, as Wilfred the Blind. He studied Kelly's legs in the forlorn hope they'd reacquaint him with himself in time to get through this speech. Her signal leer earned Peter's huge grin.

"We log into the same software," he began, waving his speech. "When I say we're looking into the face of moral decay, you know what I mean, you understand."

Mr. Speaker relaxed.

"When I speak of cultural meltdown, we're sharing the same language, and that's a comfortable feeling because we don't always hear our language on our streets any more, do we?"

He paused and was taken aback by applause. He chucked his speech over his shoulder. It somersaulted down behind him like a blasted duck.

"We are the Americans whose destiny it is to stop writing checks to cheats, to tell them to get off their duffs and work for a living. We didn't ask for the job, but it has been assigned to us, and, as patriots, we are doing it."

Even the chairman relaxed.

"We are the Americans who refuse to disarm victims for criminals, who refuse to abrogate the Constitution in behalf of the hyenas, coyotes and buzzards prowling our cities."

He definitely sounded like Peter Wattrous deGraaf. Perhaps even he could now relax. Kelly obligingly stretched out those shameless legs. He felt emboldened to speak of the usurious glories that stood before an unregulated banking industry, an unregulated economy for that matter.

"But I want to finish on the note with which I began," he said finally. "Our common language, our—we might call it our Enigma Machine—the way we have to speak so that the bureaucrats and journalists can't decipher it and even when they can, they don't know what to do about it because their interpretations won't stand up in court, so to speak."

His rhetoric wasn't parsing, but he was warming up to the subject, to say nothing of Mrs. Meyerson's legs.

"We're diverting the capital of the nation to the people who know how to use it. If some of it ends up in the Caymans or Zurich or in the hands of madmen, well, that's the price we pay for our liberties and the American way of life.

"If we stop pouring our hard-earned tax money into the sewers our cities have become, places we don't even recognize anymore, we do it for their own good, to recover our heritage, to restore our cities to the days when everybody shared them and they weren't exotic aviaries for birds of a very different feather."

The Speaker smirked.

The chairman squirmed. It was not like his son-in-law to overdo a good thing. It was Peter's turn to smile.

"We have opened our doors to immigrants wide enough. Agriculture and industry needed cheap labor. That was a no-brainer. Now we need brains. We are shifting to service industries. We must say, Only intelligence expressed in English need apply. We did not acquire Texas or California to institute Spanish as our second language, did we? And what language is spoken in our cities today? Whatever the tongue, it is very loud because a generation has arisen with a boom box on one shoulder and a chip on the other. We must, as Eliot said, purify the language of the tribe."

He cast off from Kelly's legs and scanned the room. "You know better than to applaud, don't you? But you want to. Please don't. The press is here, perhaps even *The Washington Post*, which knows the code but whose bean-counters see no dividends in deciphering it. Let's do nothing to embolden them. When their newsroom reports stagnant wages, job flight and soaring stocks, their stockholders *tsk-tsk-tsk* all the way to the bank." At this moment whimsy, as it often did, captured him. He cocked his head to hear the right bird's song, but neither the *chet-chet-chet* of the redpoll nor the *tsee-tsee-tsee* of the yellow warbler sounded quite like the *tsk-tsk-tsk* of hypocrites on the wing to the bank.

The chairman slumped in his chair, his dangling cigar sending signals up through his sleeve so that his face steamed theatrically. And Babe's porcelain chops dropped, revealing her memorable orthodontia. Stacy looked stoned. What was that girl's IQ anyway?

"We do not have to pour our gracious billions into the educational wasteland. We are using our imaginations. For starters, our prisons will pick up the employment slack. They will employ guards, nurses and the construction trades.

"We may have to squeeze the Appalachians a little, but they know why we're doing it and they approve. They know who the welfare cheaters are. They know who the criminals are. They know our agenda and that is why they helped to send the one-hundred-and-fourth Congress to Washington. They know we're taking America back. They know who from. And they know what we mean when we say moral decay, cultural meltdown, loss of the work ethic, welfare cheating.

"And I promise you, because I know this touches on what concerns you most as patriots, all this will be done before anybody invents a political lingo about tax-cheating corporations, corporate raiders who savage the economy and send millions into the streets jobless, obscene profit margins, dumbing down a population at the very moment industry needs intelligence, a Gross Domestic Product index that has nothing to do with quality of life, and all that liberal bafflegab that confuses the issue and dulls the senses."

Kelly Meyerson covered her face with her hands and shook. Babe headed for the door, Stacy in tow. Miles Richardson headed back to the bar. The Speaker stared at Peter as would the cobra the mongoose or the mongoose the cobra, Peter couldn't decide. The bilious Wallace Hyde cut a smart fart at the head table next to him. Peter turned and gave him a thumb-to-finger approval. A sandy-haired young man with a recording device in his palm swam against the pods of fleeing cetaceans to get to Peter. Kelly rose finally and brought Peter a stiff drink concocted from drinks abandoned at her table.

"Not that you need it, Peter, you did just fine without it."

He leaned over the table and embraced her. Over her shoulder, he saw the Speaker of the House of Representatives sitting alone in the Cormorant Room, his hands piously laced under his chin, watching him. When he saw Peter watching he started to approach. Kelly faded.

The Speaker took Peter's hand, wrung it warmly and for once contented himself to remain speechless. Peter still couldn't see his eyes.

That was Friday. He sailed alone over the weekend. When he returned the Babe and the Stacy had struck camp. He squinted at her note—"How could you?"—as if it were hieroglyphic. By Wednesday he was engaged in a club-foot pavane with a furniture moving estimator called by "it says Richardson here." He paused at a window in their festal home in McLean to watch the forsythia shudder in a rain-bearing east wind. He liked the forsythia's post-surgical shiver.

The phone in the middle of the living room floor rang. It was his mother from her aerie in Asheville, North Carolina.

"What are you going to do, Peter?"

"I assume you have some suggestions, mother?"

"Peter, if you have lost your mind, it can be no worse than our cousin Franklin's loss of his, can it? He ended up quite famous. In some quarters. You will land on your feet because you are equipped to do so. You have your mother's assurance about this."

He tried to keep his laughter from her. At first he succeeded. "Mother, you are so... "

"Are you laughing at me, Peter?"

"Yes, but with great love, Mother. You're so... well, you're my mother."

"Of course I am! Who else would I be? It's very unlike you to be at a loss for words. Now listen, you must remember what a marvelous hockey player you were and not give all the athletic laurels to Barbara. I know she has decamped like the athlete she is—Kelly told me—but you must call Simon Lonsdale and get him to freeze all your assets. Think, Peter."

"What makes you think I'm not?" He decided he really must visit her in Asheville soon.

"Yes, well, that was presumptuous of me, wasn't it? You're a lovely man, Peter, all one could wish in a son, I'm sure you'll do the right thing. But I must add, that is not necessarily reconciling with Barbara."

"I love you, Mother. I'm all right. Really."

He was listening bemused to life's debris fall when the chairman called him into his office Thursday afternoon.

"I'd offer you a cigar or something to drink, Peter, but you don't smoke or drink. Such a clean young man, so intelligent, what the hell happened to you? Listen, I think you should take a vacation, a little leave of absence we might call it. First Bristol owes you a rest. You've worked very hard for a long time. We're grateful. I know that if you hadn't been working so hard we would never have heard that talk about niggers and spics. Beyond the pale, Peter, I'm sure you know that. No matter what we may feel, there are certain bounds we must observe. You're a man of great sensitivity, I'm sure you understand. We have to let the dust settle, that's all. Give Babe and Stacy a little time with me. Everything will sort out."

Miles Richardson wasn't a genius, but he understood the uses of cynicism, he understood what his son-in-law had really said, he understood how it must be made to appear. But Peter deGraaf, adjusting his *fernglaser* in the chairman's face, had rounded the horn of care. He was thinking about Saint Michael and all his angels and Sidney Cohen, Dentist.

A Standing Wave

If you put a big organ in a small church you're likely to get right-angle cracks in the ceilings. Walt O'Melia is like that, organ and church. Better yet, he doesn't care. He has done the one thing he ever wanted to do. The rest happens to be what he can do. O'Melia is untroubled by hope.

That one thing glimmers forty feet high before the moon in the lobby of the Adam Petrick Tower facing Baltimore's inner harbor. The brass plaque on the marble wall says, *Black Sail, Walter F. O'Melia, 1994*. The plaque has a handle. If you pull it, you must decide either the drawer's jammed or there's no drawer.

You won't give a hoot about that little handle unless you have a mind like Walt's.

"You'd be surprised how many people come to see it," the guard tells you.

The *Sun*'s art critic failed to discover who Walt O'Melia is, so he wrote a piece that gave *Black Sail* a mystique. He culled the reference books and couldn't find Walt. Nobody told him the sail isn't always the same. Every six months Walt goes down to Petrick Tower at night and installs a different gel in front of the halogen lamp behind the sail: wine-red, turquoise, burnt umber, green.

The critic doesn't have a mind like yours. He's not going to obsess about Walt O'Melia. Like most art critics, he thinks it uncouth to share the masses' enthusiasm for anything.

Walt's not far from where you stand. He's over in Fells Point. Like a great blue heron, he stations himself here and there and waits.

If you want to know who he is, promise to be as closemouthed as the Petrick's architect. Swear you'll never tell the *Sun's* art critic or anybody else who Walt O'Melia is. Why? You want to be the sort of person who keeps a secret, don't you?

Walt loves hardware, especially marine hardware. Once he improved on slip-joint pliers, forging a self-locking one-handed tool. Years later when he saw something like it in a store he muttered, "About time."

He was making one of his frequent trips to Hartge's Boat Yard in Galesville when the black sail bore down on him like a migraine. He doesn't sail, doesn't even hanker to, he just loves sailboat gear and tackle. Maybe hearing the wind spank a just-set mainsail does it. Maybe it's spontaneous combustion. Driving home, he passes a huddle of tobacco sheds. It doesn't look as if the farmer grows tobacco anymore, so Walt crunches up the oyster shell driveway, knocks on the farmhouse door and asks if he can rent a shed for a project he has in mind.

That was Sunday. Monday he goes down to his job at Garrett Laboratories, gropes gloomily through copses of arcana in his computer, cranes his neck around a few corners and turns in a request for a leave of absence. Johns Hopkins isn't glad the world's leading standing wave researcher is pulling out of one of its projects, if only for a while, but all they can do is stand and wave.

Walt goes right to work, having been at play. His printer spews out Internet data about epoxy resins, the pot life of hardeners and their ratios to resin. He studies copper compounds and pigments. He confers by e-mail with the nation's leading fiberglass fabricators. It seems that what he's about to do is life-threatening, so he buys a respirator and protective suit. Then he buys three used genoas from Bacon's Used Sails in Annapolis. He hangs three blocks and their tackle on U bolts and shackles a sail by its head, tack and clew so that it looks capsized. He waits for fair weather and a dry breeze to keep the shed ventilated. Then he wets the sail down and starts epoxying it layer after layer day after day until it's as hard as a rock. It could have been steel or sandblasted glass or plastic, but his finicky taste demands the rough hand of sailcloth. He applies three layers of black matte paint. Finally he has a rig he likes—a sail to drive a thirty-five-foot sloop. He hauls slowly until it's almost upright. When he stands back at the entrance of the shed his jenny looks as if a hard wind's groaning in its belly.

Now he begins experimenting with back-lighting. He buys a huge theatrical lamp that can be fitted with different color gels. The first he tries is rose-hued. The jenny's burred edges gutter rose as in a dust-bowl eclipse. Walt gasps, but in an instant he's discontent. He skirts it critically for a week or two. Then he grabs a jigsaw and cuts a one-foot horizontal window into its belly just before the point where it would sweep past a mast at eye level. He spends two weeks messing about Baltimore's harbor making videos from a rented skiff. By the time he gets back to the shed in Anne Arundel County he knows just what he wants to do. When you peer into that little window you tour Baltimore's shoreline at about four knots an hour.

He doesn't want a mast. Too literal. Instead, three steel rods jut in his mind from the wall to each corner of his sail, the topmost longer so as to bear the sail down upon the viewer as if in a race. Now he wants blocks and halyards as if there were a mast and forestay, and the blocks—wooden, not synthetic—must be sanded and ambered with varnish. A white Dacron halyard must be reeved through the head block back down to a block set in the marble floor, ten unused feet flemished into concentric circles in front of the tack of the sail. Now it's finished.

It takes him about six months to refine this design to show it to Hoyt Abernathy, Petrick's architect. Abernathy is a sailor. In minutes he's talking about a wide-load flatbed truck. Walt allows himself a pleasured rictus. Abernathy's name belongs on the plaque, because it was his idea to paint a huge moon behind the sail and then work with Duron technicians for months to achieve the milky blue feldspar of moonstone.

Abernathy's inspiration gives Walt the idea for one remaining fillip: a double-convex spheroid filled with black liquid held in a clear emulsion. If he can motorize this spheroid to turn slowly before a lamp it will waft witchy shadows across the moon.

When he gets back to Garrett Laboratories he isn't interested in standing wave theory anymore. His project led him along the harrowing circuitry of his head to carbon nanotubes. Now he tells his bosses he wants to build them. They're cousins to the buckyballs named after the futurist Buckminster Fuller. Some day nanotubes will be used to build a space elevator, he says. You drop a buckytube cable from a geosynchronous orbit and it supports its own weight, unlike steel or any other known substance. Then you move materials and people, he says matter-of-factly, oblivious as usual to impressing anyone or networking, as they like to say.

"Up and down, just like that?" one of the Hopkins fund-raisers asks. Hopkins invites fund-raisers to Walt's daydreams.

"Yup, just like in a mall. Of course there are a few things to work out. Steel's primitive stuff. Think nanotubes. That's how we're going to survive earthquakes, pole shifts and the like. Remember the hoopla when solid-state electronics sent the vacuum tube to the museum? Well, the fabrication of everything as we know it is obsolete. Standing-wave technology has already turned the microchip into an artifact. That's history. Think nanotubes."

He's pretty wrapped up in conductivity tests by the time he encounters Ms. Early Ratliff. He's standing at a checkout counter in an organic food mart in Fells Point, bemused for the umpty-umpth time by the huge black clerk who calls him bubba, first because the sobriquet fits so poorly, and then because he's never heard a black man use it. The forty or so items he's picked have just stopped flashing in green digits when he feels a hard tug on his left sleeve. He turns to see a pasty-faced, scrawny young woman.

"That there total is seventy-nine dollar and sixty-two cent."

He looks at the little rectangular screen. "It says ninety-nine-forty-two."

"So you kin read," she says. "Cain't count too good, though." Her voice sounds borrowed, scratchy.

There's nobody behind her.

126

"Would you mind running it up again?" he asks the clerk.

"Same difference," the clerk says. "Gotta get my supervisor."

The young woman looks at the clerk jut-jawed. Then she looks at Walt: you want to be a fool all your life? He doesn't. He nods at the clerk. The clerk picks up his house phone and summons a supervisor.

"Numbers don't lie, y'know," the supervisor tells Walt.

This is one Walt can answer. "Hell they don't."

The clerk shoves everything back across the scanner. When he's done the screen says seventy-nine sixty-two.

The supervisor doesn't apologize, and the clerk doesn't say, See ya, bubba. Walt smiles at the young woman, gathers his bags and starts to leave. Then he wheels around, like when he spotted the old tobacco sheds, and waits for her to check out. All she has is a day-old cellophaned sandwich and a can of Mountain Dew. She's five-feet-three of scuzziness, but the way her sharp nubbins poke her T-shirt shackles his eye.

"How'd you get so good at counting?"

Her grin baits his obsessiveness as much as her peevish nipples. She doesn't think much of his question.

"Dumb question, right? I mean I'm good at certain things, but I don't know how I got that way."

This chatty O'Melia would astound his Hopkins colleagues, especially the women who worry for his health when they try to make small talk with him. But he's desperate.

"My name is Walt, Walt O'Melia. What's yours?"

"What's it to ya?"

"I'm sorry. Really. Christ, look, that guy's gonna fall off the roof if he isn't careful."

A workman festooned with tools is creeping along the ridge of the roof of the marine pier where the television show Homicide is filmed.

She stops, shields her eyes from the filthy afternoon sun and studies the situation. Walt is foolishly grateful to the workman.

"Well, if he was to drop ninety-eight feet he wouldn't splat like a egg, but he sure would feel puny."

He is savoring her hill-country speech—you get to recognize

it in Baltimore—when it dawns on him she said the man would fall ninety-eight feet if he lost his balance. Well, he figures, you could say there were five stories, each one about eighteen feet, and get the total that way, but...

"How high you figure Henderson's Wharf down there is," he says.

"Hunnerd-sixty-two feet. Ya wanna buy it?"

Nanotube elevators seem not half as interesting as this changeling. For the first time in his life he stares into a woman's eyes unaware of himself, unafraid.

"Early Ratliff. That's my name." She bites her sandwich and walks off, one thin buttock hitched higher than the other, perhaps a congenital defect.

Early, as in Earlene? Had her mother's maiden name been Early, as in Jubal? How old could she be? Where does she live? Could she be a waif? He hurts with questions, but he knows he's asked his quota. When he checks the height of Henderson's Wharf with its manager he finds that her number is half a foot off.

He doesn't have to quit carbon structure research to take on his next project, but he wants to. He had only one real ambition, to build that sail. Now he has another one, to show it to Early Ratliff. But she's gone.

He starts lurking around the Point, like a wading bird waiting for prey. He comes down there during his lunch hour, in the evening, on weekends. Drab as a sparrow, he dresses to meld with the brickwork, formstone and cobbles that characterize the Point. He has become a stalker. Then, one chill Saturday evening, three months after he begins prowling, he spots Early Ratliff rounding Fell Street and heading out on the South Ann Street wharf past the marine salvage store. He ducks into a sally port and watches. Shivering, he remembers Heisenberg's chilling dictum that observation interferes. There is no way for her to get off that wharf except by walking back, but she doesn't. He walks slowly across Thames Street onto the wharf. It is being rebuilt and there are barges alongside. No entries or alleys, no boxes or barrels, no Early. As he passes the last of three barges he hears something beat its hull. He looks down and sees a paint-splotched work platform tied to the outboard side of the barge and to the wharf. Curled up nearest the wharf is Early. She has covered herself with the white baby blanket she wears like a shawl. Early Ratliff is homeless. Or, if she has a home, it oppresses her.

He sits on the wharf until dawn, listening to lap and bump. He leaves before she wakes, but he finds her often that winter, and he comes to know every cranny, junkyard, abandoned row house, trash-can hutch and sally port in Fells Point.

He shadows Early at a respectful distance. By February he knows she feels his presence, occasionally glancing back as she turns into an alley. She knows every hidey-hole in the Point. The finer people sense her and are bereft when they don't. He sometimes watches her cover her ears against the squall of music from John Stevens Ltd. or when one of Moran's tugs blasts its horn. When anyone fails to give her a wide berth she squirms or bobs and weaves.

Walt can't think of anything or anyone he despises, except conclusions. But he is uncomfortable with most people and most things, including ideas. And he begins to notice that Early is too. He can juggle equations and data in his head indefinitely. He believes that most science is marred by people with goals. In someone with a lesser mind this attitude would be ruinous.

His profile of Early Ratliff begins to take shape when he notices that she likes the sliding doors of a big lumberyard near Little Italy. She stands enraptured in their photo beam and rocks herself from one side to another as they slide open and shut. He has read something about this, but where? He goes to the Enoch Pratt Library's Internet carrel and taps in *idiot savant*. He finds the term in disrepute. *Autistic savant* is preferred. He accesses data from the Autism Research Institute in San Diego and prints it out. Then he leaves and walks down Maryland Avenue singing *oh tidings of comfort and joy*, his hallmark refrain when he's banked something nice in his head. How prickly the autistic are—*let nothing you dismay.*

The next time he spots Early she is squatting in the doorway of a gutted building on Aliceanna Street, rocking herself. He strolls by, eating a banana, as if he's going to pass her. Then he pretends to notice her for the first time. She grins. She's on to this ruse. He holds up a second banana. She holds out her hand and opens and closes it.

"Early, what day of the week was May 22, 1961?"

"Monday," she says without hesitation.

The more he reads the more he sees the autistic savant in her—and in himself. New clothing drives them mad. Their ears are eight-quad amplifiers. People barge and encroach. They exhibit all the symptoms of post-traumatic stress disorder: if you come up behind them, they jump. Both of them calculate like computers, but Early's calendar calculations are classic.

"Whatcha got?" she begins asking him when she sees him. At first he thinks she means food, but he knows how fruitful her mooching at the back doors of the Point's restaurants is. She holds out her hands as if weighing something. She means math problems. She wants math problems.

"Early, d'you know your mind is better than mine? Really."

"So?"

Right, she's right, so what? She's more original, more daring, and much more unfathomable. He begins to give her actual carbon structure problems. She can't explain how she gets from the set-up to the solution, but whatever stumps him usually reveals itself to her.

He is now hardly ever at home on Federal Hill or at work. The two of them ramble spectrally around Fells Point. He sometimes buys food and brings it to her—she won't eat indoors. Often they eat handouts.

He never knew what his mother meant when she said, I just want you to be happy, Walt. Was this happiness?

"Are we happy, Early?"

She grins, lopsided and loony.

On a good day she can't tell how words will fall out of her mouth. Mostly they're what she remembers somebody saying back in West Virginia before she and her father got on the Greyhound and came down to Baltimore. Later that day, sitting next to Walt under a blue plastic tarpaulin spread over their burrow in a plumber's junkyard on Fleet Street, she looks up at him and waits for her words.

"Are you an angel?"

The Fake Delacroix

We see men *Tarring the Boat* in an early Manet as if we caught them by sidelong glance—but when we come up close the detail's gone. It was an impression. Nothing is what it seems. The seeming is art.

Milton Avery cuts the chop of sea before a storm into a woodblock. At ten feet the detail daunts—up close the waves look like fish bones. Down to the lichen, the specifics of his graphite-and-ink Gloucester rock arrest the eye—draw close and there's less, much less, in this less the truth.

From a distance our nation's government, its hoopla and foofaraw, impresses us as grand. We praise and damn its famous men. When you look closer you see it works when it does in spite of them, because of women, women forbearing, snatching things out of the cracks, scurrying around their offices taking care of details.

There is the impression. Then there is the craft. Travis James survived one politico after another for twenty-six years. They marched in and out like mummers. They reorganized her agency at Woodlawn so often she thought it grace it still knew its mission, to mine the Social Security Administration for statistics.

She'd come, divorced and pretty, from Albemarle, North Carolina, curious about everything and everyone. Her long relationship with a boozy reporter ended when he took a header off the Francis Scott Key Bridge.

She remembered her therapy better than her affairs. More rewarding.

She came up from Carolina with a chant every child knows haunting her, not from mocking playmates, but from Carybelle

James, her mother. When Carybelle got a chance to say no, to bamboozle and thwart, to say to her child, Them's the breaks, she chanted, *nyah nyah—nyah nyah nyah*. Not like the u-u-u lament of the Bedouin, but a nose-wrinkling glee at her child's discomfort.

The claws of this taunt savaged the girl's spirit in its infrared night.

She was long into therapy when she brought an old sepia snapshot with curlicued edges to a session one day. A pretty dark-haired woman, her legs crossed, leaned back in a lawn chaise, her expression mock bonhomie. But something was wrong, the gaze too strong, the face taut. A grave child in pigtails looked back incredulously.

"What do you think of this photo?" she asked Frank Hardesty, her therapist.

"What do you think of it?" he said, characteristically.

"Well, I'll tell you what I think," she said, "that old mother there is just sittin' in her chair fixin' to say, *nyah nyah—nyah nyah nyah*, and that li'l girl is staring at her in one hundred proof consternation, is what I think."

Frank Hardesty, a fellow Southerner who well understood the uses of dodging in and out of Southern sound and slang, said, "Travis, that ole momma has a name, so does that li'l gal, and I do believe that's a freeze frame of your life."

Travis wept. Bitterly. It seemed she wept the whole fifty minutes, Frank earning his sixty dollars handing her tissues, and when she was through, when she thought she was through, she blurted in a blast of tears and phlegm, "Well, what kinda mother would do that to an innocent child?"

Frank, an Episcopal priest, made the sign of the cross. "God loves your question, but it is yours."

She thought about taking a buyout, living on the little green yawl she'd been coddling for years at Deale, sailing and reading for the rest of her life. With Byron, her golden retriever. But when the bureau offered to buy her out for $25,000 it occurred to her it was a math test to weed out nincompoops—after taxes it left $16,000 in hand, less than a third of her annual salary.

Daddy, who wanted nothing to do with her unless she

patched things up with Momma—that's what he called his wife—was dead. Now Momma, who didn't want anything to do with her unless she promised not to talk about Daddy doing things to her, was dead too. Sort of. They don't really die. Pump buckshot into their graves, sit on your hands in Nepal, but they still hang around. Which is okay if they approved of you and loved you. But if they just pretended to and acted like you'd become misbegotten just being yourself, well, in that case you can't bury them deep enough.

Eventually Travis had a better idea. She'd let Carybelle and Wilson James hang around until they got bored. God knows she had a lot of ways to bore them. But she knew deep down that people who'd spent most of their lives in Albemarle County probably weren't going to get bored soon enough.

Once she decided to go for thirty and take all the pension she could get, she began to notice just how eccentric the mockingbird is, patrolling in the middle of the night, miming truck whine, train wail, mallard quack, even bus burp. She would climb up onto her roof deck like a submariner and listen to him greet dawn in Wolfe Street certain in his knowledge no one else had been assigned the task.

She began perching in the children's section at the Enoch Pratt Library on South Ann Street. Some of the children, the ones who got the bends coming up out of their books, would come sit next to her and share their more daunting discoveries. She whispered the words. Soon she was whispering passages and exchanging funny looks. That went on for more than a year until Bronwyn Morrison, the children's librarian, noticed that Travis was cracking up the kids mimicking the creatures in their books. She invited Travis to read to the children Saturday mornings. It was a hit.

So, at fifty-two, were not the heating and cooling switchovers in the renovated factory where she lived scheduled by a minyan, even menopause and insomnia would be sufferable. As it was, with mockingbirds' company and a Chinese fan, she managed.

She did better than that. For instance, as she was driving to a farmers' market in Bel Air one day she got behind a vintage

Buick, the humpbacked one with the worrisome incisors from the snoozy fifties, piloted by a gaffer in bib overalls and railroad engineer's cap. His wife—well, she could be his mistress or sister or both—sat like a wraith against his shoulder. He was driving everybody but Travis to distraction, so she decided to see where that was. She followed him onto Maidenhall Lane, stopped like a private eye about twenty yards off, and watched him turn into a driveway, get out, open the door for his companion and go to the trunk for whatever they'd bought.

Travis was charmed. It was so—she couldn't think what it was, so she sobbed, gratefully, then drove off reassured.

Just how much of the nation's compassion could be strained into numbers and tussled into trends—these statistics were not as reliable as the evidence of mockingbirds, old men in railroad caps and children peeing with glee at her mime's antics. You didn't have to be Travis James from Albemarle, who'd never lost the trill of her Piedmont accent, to know, but it helped. It helped her notice one night as she drove out Jones Falls Expressway a neon Christmas tree in a high-rise window on Cold Spring Lane. An unpleasant little gizmo in an unlit apartment. She had the AC on or she might not have remembered it was July. She didn't often drive at night but now she found herself going out for drives to spy that horrid little tree.

She imagined all kinds of stories, but she'd have mailed them all back to the book club. She was a teller of other people's stories. She had no inventiveness of her own, which is why one night she decided to snoop.

At first she got lost, straying into a neighborhood that had the kind of Latin bloom inveighed at by the piebald boss Ronald Reagan had sent to run her agency. The Hispanicization of the country—*Before y'know it we'll all have to yip and yak like a bunch of jungle birds*, he'd said. She'd lost a few hours' sleep trying to figure out why he'd confided this miserable little confidence to her until she woke up at four-fifteen one morning fearing it was her Southern accent. That dreadful man had confided his despicable ignorance to a lady whose Scots Confederate ancestors had abominated slavery.

She was so indignant remembering this she almost missed Northern Parkway. She maneuvered onto Falls Road, passed Cross Keys, and plumped down in a private drive in confusion when it dawned on her she might be right next to the high-rise she had been seeking. She got out and looked up the front of the building. There, eight stories up, was the awful little Christmas gizmo.

Mr. Ali Saidullah, the Eritrean engineering student at the desk, knew exactly whose tree Travis was talking about. But he wasn't about to betray her to a stranger, even a pleasant stranger.

"Well then, Mr. Saidullah," Travis said, "perhaps I could leave a note."

That passed his diligence test.

What would she say? She had Mr. Saidullah's attention. She rummaged her pocketbook for a piece of paper. Mr. Saidullah gave her a pink telephone note and a ballpoint.

"I was driving on the expressway," she began, "and when I saw your Christmas tree it made me aware I had this big sob in my chest, so I wondered why you have it there in July. It's none of my business. Please forgive me. It's just that it moved me so strangely." She signed it, then added her telephone number in afterthought.

Her note moved Mr. Saidullah when she'd gone. Something about Americans he hadn't known. They were as strange as Eritreans, as frail and human. He wished he could talk to Travis James, but he couldn't let on he'd read her note.

"Well, your note moved me as strangely as my awful little tree moved you, dear," Nita Edelstein told Travis when she called. "Would you like to come to tea?"

After that antiquarian invitation they met.

"I've gotten so nosy," she told Nita when she met her. "I seem to spy on people."

"How do you choose them, dear?"

"They do something that moves me. I start to rub this sob in my chest and then I'm in a little boat lifted by a big wave and I have to hold the tiller just right so I don't broach. But it's reassuring, that's the funny thing."

"You're becoming yourself, dear," Nita said, patting her hand. "You see, most of our lives we're so busy trying to be what we think somebody else wants us to be that we don't dare be ourselves. It's too frightening. We might displease somebody important. Then one day nobody's that important anymore."

Travis walked over to the neon tree with its chipped paint.

"I'm sure that dreadful buzzing is bad for me, but it doesn't really matter," Nita said. "It's my last Christmas tree. From the time I married Charles to his death four years ago I never had a Christmas tree because Charles was Jewish. Not a practicing Jew, but, well, one uses one's intuition. It belonged to my little friend Rodolfo. I used to mind Rodolfo while his mother Felice worked. They're from Bolivia. When they moved he gave me his Christmas tree."

Travis returned to the settee where they'd been sitting. She held Nita's hand and looked gravely into the wan little woman's eyes.

"Yes, dear, my last Christmas. God has invited me to return to the dance. I have respectfully accepted. Three more months, maybe more, maybe less. Please don't look sad, Travis. No, you musn't, because this is more peace than I've ever had. I have no further worries. I really believe that God's assurance about this is you. He has brought you to me as if to say everything's going to be all right. Perfectly all right."

They would sit in Nita's unlit apartment watching the sun irradiate the high-rises before it cauterized the city. Travis told Nita they owed these spectaculars to pollution. She explained how kerosene soot dumped by airplanes bit the fiberglass of boats near airports.

Their interest in things heightened, like a caffeine high. They enjoyed a sense of communicating with another human being for the first time. They heard each word, took each meaning, felt rewarded. They felt not so much that they'd become friends but that each of them was the first person the other had permitted to be real, to count, to matter.

Nita had spent her marriage to Charles, a research botanist for the Department of Agriculture in Beltsville, MD, abstracting and indexing everything under the sun, or a rock, for the Congressional Research Service. She regaled Travis with her favorite arcana. She began accompanying Travis to her Saturday readings. She would sit with her walker by a wall, behind the children, laughing at Travis's mimicries till she hurt.

And when the time came for the cancer to shut down her much-used brain, she said, "Isn't it surprising, Travis, that we've had no time at all to regret not having met sooner?"

Travis was to settle her estate. She would receive its residue, some fifty thousand dollars in investments, a boon to her own last days. "But what of my residue, Travis," Nita said, "what shall we do with me?"

"I could lay your ashes on the Chesapeake."

"Yes, dear, do that. That would be nice."

Before she fell into her coma and was taken to Johns Hopkins, before the inevitable question about heroic measures, she told Travis she had a gift for her in the top right-hand drawer of her dresser. Travis brought it to her on the settee and clutched it to her breast.

"It's a fake Delacroix, Travis. Do you know him?"

Travis unwrapped it and stared at an Arab horseman. She nodded.

When she had given Nita's ashes to a dark rain-bearing east wind ninety yards south-southeast of Thomas Point Light she felt so desolate she could hardly bring *Artemis* back to Deale in spite of the favorable wind.

It took a little contretemps at the main postal depot to know how desolate she felt. She'd carted five hundred press releases to the depot at nine-thirty p.m., sorted by zone and put neatly in cardboard trays, when a bearded solon of the postal service informed her that as of four weeks earlier mail stamped with the indicia of the Social Security Administration was no longer accepted—it had to be metered.

"You can mail it, but it will all be returned."

Travis stitched up her mouth zig-zag and studied the delighted beard.

139

"So does this mean the tons of stuff I mail every day is sitting in somebody's apartment with a bunch of dead animals? Because it hasn't been returned."

"Would you like to speak to my supervisor?"

"If she's a woman."

She was and she took Travis's mail. But the incident mined the depth of Travis's despair and resolved her, by one of those weird extrapolations that inspire all our better decisions, to have the fake Delacroix cleaned.

She took it to Vartan Manoogian. Study it when it's clean, she told herself. Vartan had a discreet reputation she knew nothing about as a world-class conservator. But he had problems with authority. She found him in the yellow pages and liked his name as much as his nearness. The Walters in Baltimore and a couple of curators at the National Gallery of Art knew about him and gave him work. He worked fell hours in an old glass factory in Canton across from the Exxon tank farm. It had concrete floors and he skateboarded around in it, sometimes by moonlight, engaging the ships in the harbor in a pavane.

He didn't take much notice of Travis. He cut away the brown paper backing, held the little painting to the light, looked at it askew, smelled it, then told her he'd call her with a price. Not much, he said. She took his receipt for the little fake and left her phone number.

"Missus," he said when he called, "you should come get your painting, it's done. Ninety-five dollars I charge you."

She'd feared it would be much more.

"So missus, who told you this is a fake?"

"The person who gave it to me."

"I don't think so, missus. I do a little work for the Baltimore Fine Arts. In *Who's Who* they don't put me, but a couple of these thin noses they know I'm good. They don't—whatchacallit?—authenticate paintings, which doesn't mean they can't. So I show this little beauty to a lady in the French department and she says, 'Vartan, I don't think this is a fake. You should read Lee Johnson and see if it's one of Delacroix's one hundred and fourteen lost works.' So I sit down with Mr. Johnson. Very cooperative but he talks too much. This is number one hundred and twelve. By the apprentice Mr. Andrieu it's not. They do not call it doubtful, they call it one hundred and twelve. It even has a name, *The Charge of the Caid Lamdjed*. But to authenticate it you should see a certain Mr. Inigo Darnley-Hines in New York. With such a name where else should he be?"

"London?"

"No, no, missus, they're only very English over here."

Travis's way was to brush a person's arm to signal fondness or gratitude. She did it now. But Vartan wasn't finished.

"This little picture, missus, what a story if it could talk. See, it was bigger, maybe three inches all around. Somebody cut an inch. Then this butcher wrapped what was left around a smaller stretcher. Can you imagine what a reason he had? Mr. Steven Spielberg could make a movie. Maybe it was looted or something. Somebody had to make it smaller. Who knows? For such people it is not art, it is money. This little jewel, missus, what can I tell you? It's worth a lot of money. See, under the stretcher, is the title and Monsieur Eugene Delacroix's signature. Maybe somebody wanted people to think it's a fake. See, he always wrote Eug., not Eugene. Why, how should an Armenian know?"

Inigo Darnley-Hines, his bumbershoot impeccably rolled in Travis's mind, haunted the address book in her computer for months.

Neither Byron, always up for something, tail wagging, nor *Artemis*, creaking on her lines to be under way, cheered her. In the wake of Nita's death her spiritual numbness was so deep she pinched her fingertips to make sure it wasn't physical.

But when she turned to her fake Delacroix she felt—foolish thought, she told herself—M. Eug. Delacroix had hardly succeeded until she, Travis James, studied it. She discovered it, then it earned the success it deserved. But it was not its authenticity she thought of when she claimed to have discovered it, it was its—how should an Albemarle County lady know? Ponce de Leon wouldn't have recognized it, but she did.

The Caid Lamdjed was riding a black horse left to right on a beach, leaning low behind the horse's neck, looking back. He was a southpaw, the tension of his arm, its position suggesting he'd struck a blow. Was he looking back at someone's tumbling head? It was evening, muted for a Delacroix. The gemmy quality of his paint and brush stroke was subdued. This rider had done, was doing what he was born to do and he knew it.

She thought of Frank Hardesty calling the box-camera picture a freeze frame. This was no freeze frame. This rider, this Bedouin, fully inhabited his skin, his moment, his action. For that reason it was likely that he, like Alexander the Great, had prevailed. Had the painting been lost for this very reason? Someone perceiving its truth, coveting it? But the truth was not to be tugged around stretchers, dulled by cancerous smoke, restored and reconsidered. It was something else.

Given the routine of earning a living, life ritualizes, so that by old age ritual is one's most valuable possession. One day she blocked Inigo Darnley-Hines in her computer and exiled him to its lost souls.

That same night one of her Ikea bookcases blew up. She started in bed. It was three. Books were scattershot over the room. One had smashed a vase, another a window pane. Two shelves and one of the case's sides were broken.

Like a good criminalist she left everything as it was. Three days later she saw that the book that shattered the vase was Hyemeyohsts Storm's *Seven Arrows*, a celebration of the Plains Indian way of life. And death.

From that moment, up out of her despondency over Nita's death, her puzzlement over the bookcase, her spirits rose. They rose till they soared. She stood on her roof at night singing to the mockingbirds.

Today is a good day to die—she remembered that Lakota warriors shouted it to each other—today is a good day to die. How wonderful the thought. It is what the Caid Lamdjed knew. It is what he had waited all those lost years to tell her, Travis James and no other. He did not wait for his ship to come in. He knew he was entitled to nothing. He was confounded by neither

142

his past nor his future. He expected nothing, waited for nothing, needed nothing. He did not even need Delacroix to paint him.

Today is a good day to die. The claws of her mother's taunt broke. Thank you, M. Eug. Delacroix, thank you, Vartan Manoogian, thank you, Caid Lamdjed, thank you, Lakota warrior, thank you, Nita Edelstein. She was ready to live, even if only for a moment more.

The Sandman's Art

They were helping themselves to the president, the hyenas of the House pawing their kill in the trough of the posturing boars of the Senate while the buzzards pressed and cawed. The disquietingly porcine congressor from the South was making the constitutional case against priapism when a great whim moved the glazier to crystallize the overheated bestiary, sparing it momentarily from yapping itself to death. Even the hoarse buzzards were grateful.

The ice storm made everything beautiful, but the news was the inconsiderateness of the beauty. He felt the glazier's sorrow and remembered making castles in the sand.

And when the blessed silence turned to sirens' wail, all the broken limbs and severed arteries of the former incivility lay exposed as after a quake, and even as people huddled in their powerless world, the trolls, grotesques and nyes were heard disputing their meal on The Hill.

Washington is a bad town for people who hear people think. They should avoid it. It draws them to the deafening attributes of drink. Nothing overheard in that swamp of talk emboldens the soul to transcend. Everything heard is suspect and dank.

As the fetor clawed at the ozone hole, he felt his life compress, himself jammed out. He was jogging past the power plant on the Virginia side of the Potomac. Chuff, clang, hiss, it said, and he decided then to close Others, his rare book shop on Capitol Hill. Chuff, clang, hiss. The sound of a place whose chief product is words. Yes, it would be better to put his carcass out to bleach away from the chuff of hypocrisy, the clang of rancor and the hiss of deceit. Nothing could wean these posturers from their addictions except—should he risk a thought so humble?—the prayers of the meek.

Here he could see as far as Hatteras light could reach and had as much purpose, but he couldn't discover it by naming it. When he did discover it he had no more questions in him. He'd come to do a thing too humble for words. Until his savings and his life ran out.

She noticed them four years ago. The wind erases them, the ocean drowns them, feet derange them, crabs mine them, but from Rodanthe to Salvo they appear as faithfully as tide: bas-reliefs in the sand. Octopuses with arms interlocked. A dolphin in a headset. Camelot streaming her gonfalons. He used food dye, shells, seaweed and driftwood, and nothing endured more than twelve hours.

She'd come to Salvo to die, but a dream convinced her she had a few things to do. She dreamed she was wearing a white burnoose and a cheche, one of those North African turbans. She was standing on a morning mist stirring a cauldron with an oar. I'm an alchemist, she thought. I must find proper elements.

Old age showers you with clarities and simplicities if you don't struggle. Her study of the sandman's ephemera is one of these graces. She finds them at the tide line, in the sand coves of the grass line, in the arroyo between the barrier dunes, framed by the worm-holed taffrail of a wreck, cornered by tufts of gaillardia. Her elements. Her camera her alembic, her eye its elixir.

Cordgrass binds the dunes against the wind. That's the given of the place, punctuated by ground juniper. People who look their weight in the cities and the suburbs blanch and tear loose here. In his habitual khakis he's as spectral as a sand crab. He sits so still in knurls of grass that black racer snakes feel safe to slither under his legs. He watches the sea froth, the tease of the tide, the sandpipers' daft chorus line, the phalarope's dervish whirl, families and lovers up-anchored, not as a voyeur but simply because he has learned to sit still. In the ecstasy of this gift, his face and arms streaked with green, he is moved to sculpt the sand.

Now, watching her investigate his work, as he has for more than a year, as the Croatans watched the English encroach, he sees imaginings swarm her head like gnats. He sees her heartbreak in the vulnerability of his work. He hears her stalking camera whine and snick, exulting in the capture and imprisonment of his sand sculptures.

Later, when the renters come, he sees her trophies in a gallery, his work pinned like dead butterflies. He shakes his head. Lonely as she is, as he is, she is not for him. He isn't as visible as he'd been in Washington and she's a trapper of visibilities. She doesn't know who the sculptures are for. She doesn't understand for whom he works.

That night he flies far beyond light's reach. Nothing can bring him back except the sob that wakes him.

Otley

When the heat index hit 114, when you could hear the fluorocarbons munch the ozone layer, when his eyeballs flailed in yellow goo and the Washington police cordoned the exasperated city into a maze, Otley Sprague executed Plan B.

Plan A was to retire on his modest copy editor's pension and admire girls in museums. But to his dismay private monasticism suited him better. He spent his days biking around, burrowing into the library and stalking the Internet. Until July 27, 1997. On that day he heard the poles shift and the oceans rise.

High dudgeon is the next best thing to a beer and it was better for Otley, because he'd sent too many brewers' children to college. The millennium was dithering. He'd have to hurry it. He had to untie peoples' tongues, inspire them to own the obvious. He knew as a newspaperman that politicians thrive on peoples' immunity to the obvious.

Otley was not aggrieved by Clintonian blather, congressional ruffians, our refusal to pay UN dues or the media mongers of a trash sensibility. No, he was indignant at the way we allow ourselves to be gulled by the complexity of things. He had an ancient green-eyeshade sense that things seem so complicated because they're slathered and fried in babble. Plan B which, like J. Robert Oppenheimer, he had hoped not to unleash, would change all that.

He struck first along the forty-mile Baltimore-Washington Parkway. He erected thirty black-on-white plasticized signs:

This parkway will be under reconstruction
until your government and the contractors
find a better way to line their pockets.

You would have thought aliens had landed. Motorists laid on their horns and flashed their lights up and down the parkway. The park police and the contractors scurried to remove the signs, but over an entire week the signpost phantom struck again and again.

It cost Otley a pretty penny. But his stringy old self sang hallelujah for the endorphins.

The story meetings at *The Washington Post* and *Baltimore Sun* were agonized. Everybody thought the parkway reconstruction had taken too long. And getting rid of the shoulders to install "historic" curbs was palpably stupid. But should this inciter be indulged without investigating? Did he know something reporters didn't know? And, finally, how could the newspapers ignore the glee of thousands of commuters?

While the print muses mumbled, Channel Eight struck. Now more than the parkway's users were delighted. Horns were honking and lights were winking all over the two-city region.

That's when Otley moved again. At both approaches to the part of Pennsylvania Avenue closed off in front of the White House he plastered light poles with signs saying,

Parking reserved for big shots courtesy of the taxpayers.

The very next morning Washington awoke to Manhattan's soundtrack. It seemed that every car in the city was blowing its horn. The trunks of police cruisers sported signs saying,

Honk if you like the job we're doing.

This was particular mischief, since not even the city's impervious mayor, Marion Barry, would have the gall to claim the motorists were endorsing the police department.

Not all the president's horses' asses nor all the gasbags on Capitol Hill had tickled the city's funny bone like this. People walked around giving each other a thumbs up. In a city that wined and wooed the elect, somebody, finally, was speaking for everyone else.

CNN picked it up. The nation couldn't put it down. From Maine to California, from Alaska to Florida, Otley Spragues rose up. The notion caught on faster than in-line skating, faster than navel rings or microbreweries. Otley Sprague had untied

150

peoples' tongues. They panted to shout the obvious. They discovered why the heathen rage: because they're beset with loan sharks, churning and burning brokers, fork-tongued politicians, pocket-lining preachers, medical muggers, bottom feeders, and the downright indifference of those who've gotten theirs.

Aggressive drivers apparently pose more of a crisis than downsizing predators and corporate kleptocrats. A government, a world addicted to alcohol, nicotine and caffeine spends billions warring on drugs.

Otley Sprague sat in the R Street Library carrying out his latest arcane research. Since he no longer had to edit and headline the news, it bored him. He'd said his piece. High dudgeon had lost its buzz.

Kilauea

Kilauea caught Donatella Siemens's bouquet at Saint James and shook like a cornered mouse.

"Damn!"

The rest of the day went well enough. Scripted, easy to fake. Any day she didn't have to explain her name more than once was sufferable. Her father, David Ruthven, became a seismologist and then a volcanologist largely because of a remark by his father, a garrulous vicar of Devon.

"You'd better hug the ground, my boy," the vicar said, "or the wind'll hie you away to Halifax." David liked his father's advice so much it's just what he did when he had a chance, go out to the cliffs and hug the ground. After a while the ground cleared her throat and spoke to him.

Nothing seismic was happening at Cambridge, so David Ruthven, seeing that the seismic faults in the Americas were more compelling, went off to the Krieger School of Arts and Sciences at Johns Hopkins in Baltimore, where the department of earth sciences welcomed him with a professorship. Soon he engineered a grant to study seismic phenomena along the Pacific Rim.

Kilauea counted herself lucky not to have been named Krakatoa. She suspected when her sister was christened Gemma, after the vicar's wife, that she herself was destined to be David's son. Gemma One decided Kilauea on her own career.

Her childhood visits to the vicar at Dawlish haunted her. The Rev. Ewart Ruthven had something charming to say about everything and everyone. He was an avid bird watcher. The only thing Kilauea remembered Gemma saying was, "He's the blightiest birder in history because he can't stop talking."

Gemma herself couldn't start. So of course she was the pastor and he was the preacher. He never seemed to notice that while his parishioners loved him they went to Gemma for advice, which they never got, because Gemma said so little, but they came away anyway thinking everything settled.

Kilauea loved Gemma madly. Her grandmother had fire-thorn hair and blue fairy eyes. When she died Kilauea, then eleven, erupted, "She's not dead at all, you know, she's just decided it's more fun dancing with the fairies!"

She believed it. Her decision to become a musicologist, rather an historian of musical instruments, had somewhat to do with her father David's ear to the ground, but mostly it had to do with Gemma's playing the viola da gamba barefoot in her nightgown. There were certain places in the floors of the vicarage—always where light poured in—whose resonances she liked and that's where she played.

Kilauea's days dawned between Gemma's legs, sang to the sexual buzz of reverberant wood and bone, danced in summer heat and white light, basked in long fey smiles and that off-world gaze. She knew no sentient being, having seen Gemma that way, could have believed she died. Such a being leaves.

If Gemma's son wished, she would bear the name of a dangerous volcano.

***

"What did you mean, darling?"

"Mean?"

"You know," her mother Martha said, "when you said damn. Such an odd thing to say, dear."

"Well, I don't know, Mother."

"Pity your father's not here," Martha said distractedly. "He would've known what you meant, wouldn't he have?"

"Yes, I suppose he would have."

Martha was always behind the curve, gamely trying to catch up. It was only the second Gemma she didn't have to catch up to. Martha and her younger daughter understood each other perfectly. True, they might have to admit, there is evil in the world, but it doesn't have to interest them, does it? Kilauea would never have survived her mother and sister if she hadn't the memory of her grandmother's smile to buoy her.

"You caught it! What does it mean, Lauea? Do you have a secret admirer?"

Gemma Two was not unlike their grandfather.

Kilauea regarded Gemma Two, six years her junior, gravely. She leaned over and kissed her. Then she handed her the bouquet.

"Lauea!"

"I pass, Lovey."

***

Martha considered it her most creditable achievement to have said something at last that amused Kilauea so much it forged a bond between them where none had been. It was soon after Donatella's wedding in Kilauea's twenty-ninth year.

"Darling," Martha began in her usual stammer, the one that disarmed everyone but her oldest daughter, "you know what a compulsive housekeeper I am. I just have to touch everything with a cloth or a duster. Well, there's your father's urn, you see. I'm afraid that I'll just grab it some day and start polishing it and he'll reappear, all smoky with huge pointy ears."

Her mother's sense of humor, so fastidiously hidden all these years, dynamited Kilauea's Scots reserve. She fell on her mother, shaking with laughter.

"You're such an awful housekeeper, dear," her mother continued, on a roll, "I know you won't touch it—him. So, you see, I'll feel safer... "

She put her forefinger on her mother's lips, went to the mantelpiece and took the urn.

Of course it wasn't just Martha's humor that emerged. She thought that with David Ruthven in his son's hands, so to speak, she might just get on with the rest of her life. And she thought Kilauea was too focused on her scholarship to guess. Besides, the family might joke about Kilauea being the only son, but Martha knew Kilauea was Gemma's child. She knew it when she first laid eyes on her. The girl never bawled, she just looked into her

155

mother's eyes. "It's you, is it? Well, I guess you know I'm none too happy to be here, but we shall have to make the best of it, won't we?"

***

The urn worried Kilauea too. It didn't belong. She started writing to English musicologists to see what she could turn up. Then she decided to go to Dawlish, where Ewart had told David to hug the ground. She'd just let him ride the wind to Halifax. Maybe she'd hire a bagpiper. The Ruthvens were Scots, but they'd lived in Devon since the Plantagenets—they had probably irked some Scottish laird who wished them on their fellow zanies, the English.

She rented a car at Heathrow and drove to Dawlish. She had no idea what to do, nobody to see, nothing to look up, not in Devon anyway. Standing by the sea in khaki shorts, her denim shirt and red hair sounding in the wind, she thought she might just reach into her knapsack, give David's ashes to the wind and go to Oxford, where she was bound to learn something at the Ashmolean.

She was thinking of doing just that when a white sail about a mile out flashed in the sun. The boat was crossing Lyme Bay almost due west on a starboard tack so that she could see two masts. Kilauea was a good sailor. She had been drawn to boats not by the sea but by their tackle and gear. Her scholarship infatuated her with objects. This boat, being two-masted, would be a schooner, ketch or yawl.

But it wasn't.

Kilauea's eidetic mind leafed through Jane's and half a dozen other ship-recognition manuals. It stopped at a UNESCO paper on Turkish musical instruments. While she had been reading that paper she had amused herself over a bag lunch with another treatise on Arab shipbuilding.

Now she leafed through it mentally. Dhow—that was the generic word. Ghanjah, baghala, boom, zarook—she was looking at an Arab boom. She wished she'd brought her binoculars. But her eyes were good. It was not only a boom, it was a swift double-ended boom, its lateen sails raked back, its shrouds blocked, its bowsprit pointed jauntily up and carrying a small headsail, a long green burgee streaming from its stern. She could even see a figure in white shoving against her huge tiller.

Ridiculous. She shut her eyes, rubbed them, then opened them wide and refocused. She looked from side to side and behind her. Then she looked at the sailboat again. The wind had freshened. It was closer. It was an Arab boom.

She laughed. This is the asylum of eccentrics, Kilauea. Some joker, maybe even a Ruthven, has fashioned himself a boom and is putting on everyone off the Devon coast. It's a pricey send-up.

Dawlish benefited from her smile. She started down the road toward a church spire, leaving the little yellow Austin where she'd stopped.

Saint Columba's looked towards Teignmouth and the channel, lumpen, wet-shaped by giant thumbs. Kilauea entered the narthex, waiting for her eyes to adapt. When they did they saw a puzzle. Two elderly women arranged flowers on the altar, passing the altar to and fro with nary a wee Catholic nod. On the other hand, a red-lit lamp, the reserved sacrament, hung over the communion rail. Such things might elude Presbyterian notice, but Kilauea was born to this church and such things interested her in any case. She decided to tap the wood with a fingernail, pluck a string or two, so to speak, so she advanced down the aisle, stopped at the transept and coughed for their attention. When she got it she genuflected just to see what would happen. One of the women nodded at her unhappily and after that they bowed as they passed the altar. Her ruse had flushed them out. It was, after all, a high old church where Anglican manners might gutter a bit on a windy Devon hill. Pleased, Kilauea entered the front pew, crammed an embroidered kneeler under her knees and bowed. Later she sat upright looking around, studying a comb of organ pipes in front of their loft, taking in the choir stalls. She was the sort of person who couldn't imagine living where she hadn't identified all the trees.

"Excuse me, dear, we normally lock up when we're done. We didn't used to, but these days..."

"My name is Ruthven. My grandfather was vicar here. Did you know him?"

"Oh yes! Dear, dear Father Ruthven... why, you must be Kilauea. Of course! I remember you when you were a child. You used to clutch your granny's dress and follow her everywhere. Where are you staying, dear?"

She explained that she had just arrived, was a historian of sorts and was here to study and to bear her father's ashes home. The women vied to invite her to stay with them. They said she must meet the vicar. Everyone would want to meet her. She said that for the moment she would like to sit there and compose herself.

"Certainly, my dear," Mrs. Truscott said, "here is my key. Just lock up when you're ready. I live two houses down the road on the left, the one with the widow's walk. Take all the time in the world, dear. We're so happy to see you." Mrs. Davenport stood a foot or two behind, nodding.

When she was alone Kilauea inventoried the two brass low mass candles, the gilt tabernacle on the altar, the bad icon of Saint Columba, the green frontal, the bell by the sacristy door, the weary reredos with its glued-together icons, the lady altar to her left where the mother of God looked down, palely English.

Beyond the ogee doors of the west nave she heard Gemma playing. She closed her eyes and saw her. She listened a long while. Why, she wondered for the first time, had Gemma and Ewart had only David? She dared more. Had Gemma a lover or two? Who would not fall in love with her, man or woman? Ewart?

She rose, climbed the chancel steps, bowed her head and entered the choir stall on the gospel side so that now Gemma was behind her. She sat still in the back stall. Over her head was the mirror in which the epistle-side choristers watched the organist direct them. Entering from either side of the narthex, you would not have seen her behind the rood screen.

A gull bombed the slate roof with a shell to crack it and eat its secret. Other gulls palavered. The wind rattled the downspouts. Beneath their lids Kilauea's eyes rolled up in Anglican samadhi.

Her wrists rested on her thighs, her left thumb tucked into her right hand. Her knees were wide apart, like Gemma's. Sweat traced fondly the crescents of her breasts. Rivulets joined, rose in her navel, flowed over and down to what she now remembered Gemma had called her depot stove.

She was smiling to remember this when the doors of the east nave opened. White shapes barged in. Guttural shouts. Flashes of steel. Scuffling. Women screamed, babies squalled. Kilauea stared through the rood lattice. Where had the women and babies come from? A loose-limbed man in black raced down the center aisle. "I implore you..." he was saying. His biretta fell. He staggered and toppled back over a pew.

Kilauea saw the pale women and their pink babies clearly. They wore caps, drawstrings awry. She saw shapes spank and flash in roars of sun. She clutched the lattice, intent as a moviegoer annoyed by chatty neighbors. Women raced down the side aisle pursued by—they were corsairs. She recognized their djellabahs and burnooses, twisty headdresses, wicked sabers.

She believed, had believed for a long time, if you studied a thing long and hard enough, if you concentrated like a Zen archer, it would tell you what it wanted to become. She knew a suicidal bassoon. Certain gardens showed her their opinion of gardeners, berserking themselves for her eyes only, rearranging themselves, or, like Monet's, applauding like children. Leaf curl, wood gnarl, grain ding, finger oil—the numerousness of life— these held Kilauea in rapt remove from the weather of feelings. She was always in conference. To be her friend, to even start, you must sit still and bear contemplation. Not because Kilauea was judgmental, she wasn't, but because her nature was to consider. Like a night heron.

She did that now.

Some chemical switch. You grope in the mind's dark and there it is. You don't know what it is, but it's better than the dark. It could be the burglar alarm, yard lights, corsairs. She squeezed her eyes shut as she'd done as a child to turn streetlights into seed-heads of dandelion. When she opened them neither the corsairs nor their victims had blown away like seeds.

Always wound to sprint, for which reason she made a sought-after grinder in yacht races, Gemma's child bounded out from behind the screen.

"What are you doing? You, put that baby down! Put it down, I said!"

If you had looked closely—somebody soon would—you would have seen Gemma smile sidelong on Kilauea's face. She entered into the thing for the fun of it—the worst that could happen is that it was real, that the church had not only given up one of its stories to her, it had pulled her back into it.

How very odd, she thought, even while trying to impress the corsairs with her authority. What an amazing reward for her reverence of things, she thought. No wonder Ewart Ruthven spent most of his life fretting about just who Gemma worshipped.

Rosie Grier in operatic turban pinned her arms. Her fanny bounced on his belly, her legs flailed. Rosie laughed like the bowels of—Kilauea.

"What have you done with my knapsack, you dipshit!"

Rosie keelhauled her around and held her up to his face. She aimed for his jewels but kneed too high. He smiled as if he'd made a friend. He grabbed her hair and turned her out to face—she wanted to think him the handsomest man she'd ever seen, but that hardly suited the man she saw. He tickled her throat with the point of his scimitar and cowed her pale blue eyes with the wildest blue eyes she'd ever seen. His face was bronzed and hawkish, his beard black and pointed.

They stood there, the three of them, Kilauea dangling in Rosie's arms, the corsair captain—he was clearly their commander—feathering her throat with steel and contemplating her. This frieze shattered finally when she considered his mouth. Its fine lips were pursed, like an archaeologist's or a surgeon's. She smiled, slow, even, pleased. He turned his beautiful head to regard her out of the corner of an eye, hoping by this to fathom an infidel's smile. Her eyebrows lifted quizzically. The captain's fierce face creased crazily in a smile of pure delight. He nodded. Rosie put her down. The captain returned his scimitar to its filigreed scabbard. He locked an elbow over a wrist, put his mouth between thumb and forefinger and considered her. Then he did it, the thing Gemma could never resist—he gently smoothed back the rebel cowlick at the side of her head. He nodded several times, then turned and left, his men behind him. The women they pushed off, the babies they set down. They took nothing, no one.

She heard them sing outside. Then only the sea thrashing.

She went back to the choir stall and sat again behind the screen. Only then she thought to look down to see what she was wearing. Would it be high black shoes and a long dark dress? She wore her Vasque hiking boots, her khaki shorts and denim shirt.

Had Gemma seen them? Was he Gemma's captain? Her breasts wanted room. She pulled her shirt forward delicately. Only then she knew that not in the back seats of cars or anywhere anytime had her secret parts answered another's call so boldly.

It was a reverie. That's all. Wasn't it? But she couldn't shake her sense that a door had opened and shut. She could not have stayed the corsair captain, could she have? What might she have done differently? It was reverie. That was all she could bear for it to be, all it could be.

Get over it, find Mrs. Truscott, poke around the Ashmolean. Outside nothing antique plied the sea. She set off down the road.

***

Day after day she sat barefoot in a high-backed chair in Hartoft Mews in Oxford, playing a borrowed viola da gamba. The E-string was raw, the G buzzed. She sanded the pegs, adjusted the fingerboard. Her fingertips hurt from the pizzicati. But she played with the fanaticism of a body builder.

Oxford held no charms for her, except the afternoon when she decided she owed it to herself to finger the eighty parts of a Gagliano violin she'd been told about, or the morning she studied corsairs.

They'd bedeviled the English coast for four hundred years. Their last recorded raid was probably whispered in Elizabeth Tudor's ear. They carried off men, women, boys, girls, babies, and whatever of value they could lay their hands on. They scrawled iconoclastic graffiti on church walls. The children of Wessex, Devonshire and Cornwall scanned the horizon for them long after the infant U.S. Navy forever doused their ardor.

She wondered what Joy Halvorsen at Hopkins would think. It was down Joy's alley. A neurological researcher and Jungian psychiatrist, Joy Halvorsen was working on a book on the effects of certain musical instruments on the brain. Kilauea had promised to map the provenances of the instruments. She should call Joy. Joy was not hostile to parapsychology.

All she wanted to do was play. In the wood, in the bone— the words came to her every time she decided on a course of action. To dress, to eat, to go out, to call somebody. In the wood, in the bone, that's all she could think. Weeks passed. She ate in the evening, grabbing a sandwich and walking through the ancient streets. In the morning she started playing again.

Then one morning she called Joy Halvorsen, apologized, said she'd finish her vignettes and get them off, bought a ticket and packed. Whatever she had been doing, she was finished with it. She wasn't interested in going home to Monterey. It was home because David had left her a house.

She thought she was leaving her fugue state in Hartoft Mews, but on the plane she opened her knees and her bones sang the chords of Gemma's viola. She smiled slowly at the window. All right, this is going to be quite a trip.

***

Gemma Two had news on Kilauea's second night back home. "You must meet him right away, Lauea. I told him if he can't pass muster with you, he's dead. He's dying for me anyway. Really. I can't believe it. He's so gorgeous. Well, not Hollywood gorgeous, but—he's kind of exotic, Lauea. Oh, please let me bring him over tomorrow. And be nice, Sis. Okay?"

"I'm always nice, Gemma. It's just I'm distracted sometimes. What does this exotic do? Oh, I'm sorry, Gemma, forget I said that. I hate it when people ask what I do. You tell them and then that's what you are—what you do."

"He's a merchant seaman. A navigator. I don't know if I can deal with that, Lauea. But he's wild about me. What can I do?"

"And you're wild about him?"

"Sis, I've had lots of friends and I've never brought them to you to inspect."

"Mmm, this must be serious. Well, tomorrow then. I'll make us lunch."

***

"When the sun dies it will boil the seas and our very arrogant gooses will be cooked."

"Geese, Father, our arrogant geese will be cooked."

She remembered this conversation because it happened here on the front porch where she sat now waiting for Gemma and her sailor. She sat propped against a post, balancing her coffee on her knee.

Our geese... Gemma's little MG, which she endlessly tuned and fiddled with, pulled up hard and Gemma jumped out. "Lauea," she called, running up the walk. Kilauea got up and came down the creaky steps, noticing Gemma's sailor taking his time.

"Sis," Gemma said quietly, hugging Kilauea. They hugged. Kilauea watched the sailor, her chin resting on Gemma's shoulder. His face was bronzed and hawkish, his beard black and pointed. He had the wildest blue eyes she... He gazed at her solemnly. He pursed his lips and then he raised his eyes from her infidel smile to consider her rebel cowlick. He wanted to touch it. She remembered.

"Let me look at you," Gemma said. She held Kilauea by the shoulders. But Kilauea's eyes were shut.

Night Pass

Paolo Maio heard God say, Stop, listen. So he took a walk thinking if God had any decency at all he'd elaborate.

Paolo's mother, Laura, had often watched him sitting in his crib turning his head like a satellite dish. What's he listening to? What does he hear? Today Paolo wondered if listening is good for an artist.

He considered the paraphernalia of others' lives as he walked along the Fells Point waterfront in Baltimore. His mind took snapshots as he loped: snatch blocks of seamen, graven signs of bars, star studs clamping slumping walls, swollen teenagers with shiners and snaggled teeth.

Paolo's eyes served his secret ear. He heard things speak. His nature and mien moved people to say strange things to him, encrypted things. He preferred the words of objects natural and made. These had no cunning.

Only God presumed on Paolo's listening. God with his crazy orders. Perverse, laconic, comedic God. Stop, listen go, wait, what's going on here? how do you feel? watch out. God spoke to Paolo when he damned well pleased, and it was no use for Angel Cardenas, Paolo's therapist for four years, to try to convince him this is a man's interior dialogue, the brain's technique.

No, Angel could chip at his grandiosity until the media duly noted the Second Coming and the Lord had his interview with Charlie Rose, and Paolo would go right on hearing God, bemused and annoyed.

"Didja get a good look, sucker?"
"No, whud-eye miss?"

A raptor-blonde about as tall as Paolo, which was six-two, hovered out of the August heat maze looking as if Hieronymus Bosch had painted her, flailing in a man's shirt, Orioles' cap backward. She hauled up short abeam, zonked by his absentminded retort.

"You crazier'n I am, sucker."

Paolo smiled shyly, liking the sound of it. "Whuddya mad at?"

"You, Mother!"

Paolo peered into her caged eyes, savoring the wily stupidity of his question.

"I'd like to paint you. Then..."

"Nobody messes with me, mother."

"I don't want to mess with you, I want to paint you," he said.

"With what?"

He liked that question so much he laughed.

"With paint."

He wanted to say something better but he couldn't think what.

"You son of a bitch, I oughta beat your ass."

"Well, I might let you do it if you let me paint you."

Portraits weren't his thing. And certainly not messing with angry women, but there was something so lovingly disordered and yet inevitable about her that it excited him. She was as forbidden as a child.

He saw a fey smile tease the right corner of her thin mouth, the crooked abused girl-child's smile that gets caught between the ears of daddy's drinking pals. He was in any case a sucker for crooked smiles and bowed legs.

"So where d'you live?"

"I got a loft up Broadway a few blocks."

"You really paint pictures?"

"I don't lie."

She looked carefully around his ear, then off into space.

She looked as if she'd stick around her weird thirties until she was an old crone, one of those people, once seen, you can't imagine the world without.

"See my aura?"

"Yeah. It's okay. I'd scrub it up a bit."

166

"Who'd scrub it up?"

"I meant you. If I were you."

"So then what color would it be?"

"Pale yellow."

He said he didn't lie. Now that was a lie. Her aura was golden, no flecks or flickers. Pure gold. He was dismayed he'd lied.

Anybody who had anything crazy to say said it to Paolo. They were like foreign speakers falling on one of their own. His big yellow eyes and tow-haired aspect drew the eye off his leery stoop, his surprisingly sharp cheekbones and thin mouth. Paolo wasn't handsome, he was magnetic. Especially around trouble.

Paolo broke Lise van Tuyl's concentration. Bag ladies are concentrated. Having access to his loft disturbed her. She could raid his fridge, use his bath and store bags in his storeroom if they didn't smell. It proved difficult to punish him for this, so she washed up one day and seduced him. That is to say, he accepted the invitation.

They were childish lovers. To each other at least. That puzzled them. She wished to hurt. He wished to be kind but casual. That's not what happened.

Paolo was a good cook who often forgot to eat. He resented having to. Most people who resent it cook badly or not at all. But Paolo took pride in doing what he did well. He especially resented eating when God said something frolicsome.

So Lise's comings were welcome because they moved him to nurture. He sketched her many times. But he couldn't paint her. It was as if she had not been wholly made and he wasn't going to take the responsibility. Parts of her didn't want to be painted but they did condescend to be drawn. She bitched a little, but she figured once he'd painted her she'd be less than welcome, so she shut up about it.

He'd never met a human figure didn't want to be drawn. He'd grunt and swear, break pencils and charcoal, walk around splattering sweat, tell her to take a break when he didn't want her to, get mad and walk out leaving her there naked. But he couldn't tell her what was wrong because he knew it would freak her worse than him. Or if it didn't, it'd give her power over him. Or maybe both?

Paolo follows through on his enthusiasms. But now one of them gets the best of him. He leaves off doing big geometrics into which he sets miniature landscapes and cityscapes and begins to haunt the city with holograms. He becomes a guerrilla holographer, hunted by the cops, celebrated by contrarians and the downtrodden.

One night, for example, he projects Che Guevara's face on City Centre. He follows up this stunt with Nat Turner's face on the famed Bromo Seltzer Tower, and then, deciding not enough people recognize the slave rebel, he projects the face of Martin Luther King Jr on the tower.

On the most pretentious banks he projects the faces of Jesse and Frank James, Bonnie and Clyde, and John Dillinger, whom old-timers mistake for Thomas Dewey.

On the homes of the filthy rich he lasers the wide-eye face of Emiliano Zapata and Subcomandante Marcos, peasant patriots of Mexico.

He turns the city into a mobile museum. Cesar Chavez, the Berrigan Brothers Daniel and Philip, Harry Bridges, the longshoremen's onetime fiery leader—all burn themselves into Charm City's consciousness as Paolo aims his split laser beams at select targets.

The *Baltimore Sun*, in spite of its stodgiest instincts, hails him as a major artist and advises the police department to spend its money more wisely. A *Sun* editorial even speculates that H.L. Mencken, once the *Sun*'s famously crabby columnist, would have delighted in Paolo's daring, if not his choice of champions.

But Paolo, as usual, is working on a quandary: how to project six images of his champions in syzygy, like a rare lineup of planets. Which champions? How much equipment? Which buildings?

God let him execute this project uninterrupted. He'd never let him work more than five minutes on a painting without delivering what Paolo called a loonygram.

"I think you have to do what you fear. Is that it? Goddamn you, is that it?"

"Join the Foreign Legion? Goose a nun? Is that what you mean?" Angel had asked.

"I wasn't talking to you," is what he wanted to say. "Don't be an asshole, all right?" is what he did say. "What I'm telling you is I think fear is a sign pointing to where we have to go."

"So whuddya fear?"

How could Paolo tell the truth, that he feared exactly what he'd been doing all his life? Listening. "I'll let you know," he said.

"Paolo, Paolo, I fear for you, my son," young Angel said. "I mean, d'you sleep with a woman infected with HIV because you fear?"

"Angel, your hearing's so selective I wonder if you're in the right business."

"It's all right to talk to yourself, but when you start believing your answers it's time to start shoveling."

Paolo had whoofed many a charcoal crumb off his pad musing how Angel would look if he told him God had been importuning him. He'd given Angel some bait when he'd said, "I suppose it's okay for Oral Roberts to talk to God, especially about money, but it's not okay for artists who God knows need the money more than Roberts."

Angel said nothing. After saying nothing for a long while at seventy dollars an hour, he said, "You strike me as more verbal than visual." Paolo knew when Angel wasn't working for his money.

"No, I'm more a-u-r-a-l than Oral, Angel."

"Proving my point," said the caught-out therapist.

Paolo once gave Angel a small painting for Christmas. Angel said nothing, not even thank you. Paolo wasn't offended, he was intrigued. He knew two things for sure: he painted well and God's a provocateur.

Paolo harbored what he called the Florentine Hunch. His hunch was that we all hear God and know much more about each other than we can bear to admit. He imagined that if he ever told Angel this, Angel would say either that it's a social pact to keep us civilized or it's a Maio special. It keeps us uncivilized, is what Paolo thought.

Angel would not approve of Paolo's relationship with God. God on the other hand approved of Angel. Paolo thought it was little enough God could do for a man called Angel Cardenas. Paolo's God was not so much curmudgeon as stoic, not so much stoic as beset. He seemed beset by things his creatures couldn't fathom. That was his grandeur.

Paolo once dreamed the universe is the great Mexican clown Cantinflas looking like an ox beset by gnats and fleas. In what field then does God the oxen universe stand twitching his hide? That and like questions almost drove him mad. He drew that dream till he drew it clean out of his head.

He met Lise walking off God's instruction. God knows who else he'd meet trying to figure out what God wants him to hear. It had something to do with fear, he was pretty sure. But maybe it had to do with how one handled fear.

"With style," Paolo thought smugly one day. "That's it, you have to handle fear with style."

But surely God preferred substance to style. Then Paolo thought of the Renaissance masters whom he loved, including the obscure Lavinia Fontana of Bologna. They had substance and style. Aha! he thought. But aha what?

His walks continued.

He ducked one night into a gelato shack on Thames Street and, spading a plastic spoon into a cardboard cup, he crossed a narrow street onto Fells Point's broad brick piazza where deals went down, drunks slept and bands oomp-pahed, polkaed and mariachied according to the ethnic flavor of the week. He perched on the back of a slatted bench.

A graying black man in bib overalls appeared from behind and poked his forefinger and pinkie at Paolo's eyes. Paolo did not blink. The man wore no shirt. His hair was plaited in Rasta dreadlocks.

"You got de night pass, mon?"

"No," Paolo replied pleasantly, "somebody thought it was a credit card and stole it."

The man was mock-impatient.

"No, mon, you suppose to say, A what?"

"Oh, all right. A what?"

"Night pass be what de Boer say de black mon need to hab in de city at night."

"The who?"

"De Boer."

"Oh, you're talking about apartheid."

"No, mon, de Boer be scare of de boogeymon."

"What are you scared of?" Paolo asked.

"De boogeymon."

"Who is the boogeyman?"

"You de boogeymon."

Paolo liked this idea.

"Want some gelato?"

The man shook his right hand sideways.

"Lemme see if I get you," Paolo said, "the boogeyman stands guard over what we fear. I mean, I look down a street and I get the chills because I know the boogeyman is there. Right?"

"Sound good, mon."

Paolo now regarded the man warmly. "I'm Paolo. What's your name?"

The man allowed the theatrical interval.

"Legion."

Paolo burst into laughter, spluttering his red gelato at Legion.

Legion waited for Paolo to compose himself. Then he started shuffling backward chuckling. It sounded as if a fissure in the earth had opened.

Paolo watched and it came to him this is what God meant.

The man kept backing and when he was about three yards off he said, "Remember, mon, you put de marga in de pot and then you put the cous-cous on top."

Paolo put down his gelato. Then he put his face in his hands and thought to laugh, but he couldn't tell if he was laughing or crying. Then he remembered a Bahamian sailor who called the auxiliary diesel of a sailboat an ox.

"Hey, Legion, remember, no ox, you be get dere slow!"